SUGAR AND SLICED

A SMALL TOWN CULINARY COZY MYSTERY

MAPLE LANE COZY MYSTERIES
BOOK 0.5

C. A. PHIPPS

M.L.M.

To all my family members and those friends who think what I do is a hobby and I sit at home drinking coffee all day and playing on the laptop with my dog snuggled beside me so I can't get up.

Okay, some of that is true.

SUGAR AND SLICED

A Manhattan bakery, a boyfriend blunder, a combative contestant, and almost crushed by a body!

When a body lands at her feet, the death is literally too close to home for Maddie Flynn. The baker with more than a recipe or two up her sleeve is thrown into the investigation when things don't add up with the crime. With his uncanny sense of who is good and who isn't, even Big Red, her larger-than-life Maine coon, is seeing things in the shadows.

Not everyone is happy with her digging, so there's a chance she may end up the next victim if she can't solve the murder soon. And what does an angry contestant have to do with a kidnapping?

If you love Murder, She Wrote, you'll enjoy Maddie's style because she's not taking no for an answer either.

The Maple Lane Mysteries are light, cozy mysteries featuring a quirky cat-loving bakery owner who discovers she's a talented amateur sleuth.

Each book contains an easy recipe!

5* "This story was a quick, easy read with a good pace, crime with a taciturn police detective trying to hold Maddie in check, and a baking competition that turns triumph to terror! Big Red, Maddie's Maine Coon cat companion, is a mighty protector prowling the streets of NYC and a key player. I love a cozy with a sassy pet."

The Maple lane Mysteries
The Maple Lane Cozy Mysteries
Sugar and Sliced - Maple Lane Prequel
Apple Pie and Arsenic
Bagels and Blackmail
Cookies and Chaos
Doughnuts and Disaster
Eclairs and Extortion
Fudge and Frenemies
Gingerbread and Gunshots
Honey Cake and Homicide - preorder now!

Join my mailing list to find out about new releases and deals on my books.

CHAPTER ONE

The large ginger Maine coon sat huffily by the door glaring at her.

"I'll see you right after work," Madeline Flynn promised. "Then we'll go for a long walk before it gets dark."

Big Red slunk away to the small window and turned his back on her. It was 4 a.m., so there was little chance he could see anything outside, but as an adept sulker this was his go-to position. To be fair, he had every reason to be fed up. Not only did she wake him with her early starts, he was also alone most of the day. The was what bothered her most. Big Red was a very social cat—when he wanted to be.

Maddie sighed, grabbed her thick coat, gloves, and scarf from the stand by the door, and left him to his bad mood. She paused on the small landing to wrap up tight and study the first door up the next flight of stairs. Last night she'd heard muted voices in the apartment above her. It may have been her imagination, but she'd thought her neighbor was arguing with someone.

Cleo Black was polite when they occasionally saw one another and looked to be in her late twenties, the same as

Maddie. Other than a brief hello, Cleo didn't encourage conversation, and Maddie knew nothing about her except her name, that she was attractive and had a penchant for dark clothes. The argument, if it was one, didn't go on for too long, so there was probably nothing to worry about. Although, that never stopped her before.

Shaking her head at this need to fix things, she walked quickly through the darkened streets of New York, pushing down the flutter of anxiety. The city was a long way from Maple Falls, the quiet hamlet where she'd been born and raised, and seemed like another world. From the amount of people to the smells and sights, it had been an assault on her senses for at least the first month after she moved here fresh out of college.

A few years on, she still missed all the green and quiet, but there was so much to see and do in a city this size. Things she never dreamed of. Like ice skating in Rockefeller Center or shopping in Chinatown for hours to find special ingredients or ones she'd never seen before. Plus, there were restaurants for every kind of cuisine on the planet.

With a self-imposed and necessary budget, Maddie relished the challenge of finding a filling and tasty meal for as little as she could spend. It was fun, even if she only had Big Red to share in the adventures.

Another sigh escaped her lips as she crossed the street. Arguably, her boyfriend Dalton should have been her companion, except he hated food that wasn't served on China. If he occasionally took her to a nice restaurant, she might feel more charitable at his snobbery, but they usually ate at her apartment—which meant she cooked. After working in a bakery since before sun-up, Dalton loving her cooking wasn't enough for her to want to do it every day. A sandwich eaten snuggled next to Big Red on the couch would be enough for her.

Maddie wrapped her scarf tighter. Moaning about Dalton, if only to herself, was becoming a way of life and certainly no way to start the day. Fortunately, the small apartment she'd managed to rent was only a few blocks from where she worked at a French bakery with her friend Camille. When she turned into the main street, Christmas lights hanging from the storefronts and trees made everything brighter and less dreary. She loved Christmas and so did Big Red. Those lights and decorations were a huge temptation for an inquisitive feline.

Up ahead, the even-brighter lights of the bakery welcomed her and as usual soothed her troubled mind. It didn't open for another hour, but the three uncles who owned and ran it, including Camille's father who Maddie always called Uncle Joey, would already be hard at work mixing dough for bread to give it time to rise and bake before the first customer arrived.

She hurried down the alley beside the shop's brick facade and entered through the back door. Camille grinned at her over the huge barrel of a mixer.

"Morning, Maddie," Uncle Joey called to her from a table near the door, while the other men nodded and smiled. Camille's father was the youngest of the brothers and the most fun.

"Good morning, everyone." Always early, Maddie tucked her bag and coat into a locker then slipped on a clean apron. Eagerly scanning the board listing tasks for the day, which was always a little exciting, she grinned at the slices on her list to bake. Maddie loved making the layers, ensuring each one was perfect in size and look when finished. Each rectangle should tantalize before the taste delivered on the fantasy.

Everyone had their own station and hers was as pristine as when she'd left it yesterday afternoon. She lined up all the ingredients on her left except for the flour and sugar. These were in huge tubs, situated centrally, which were far too heavy to move.

She took a large mixing bowl over to them and using the scoop hanging from the rim measured out the sugar. Next came the butter, which was stored in plastic tubs. Creaming the two together using one of the large mixers until they were light and fluffy, she separated the eggs and beat in the yolks. Next she added sifted flour and baking powder and stirred until combined.

Recipes in the bakery were often several times the amount a home cook would use, and by the time she was done stirring her arms ached a little. Where possible the work was done by a mixer, but some stages required a lighter touch. In the beginning she'd found it incredibly hard, but eventually she became stronger, and it was less arduous.

Now she pressed the dough into a large, greased tin and spread a thick layer of strawberry jam over it until it was completely covered. Lastly came a meringue mixture, made by beating the egg whites until stiff then adding sugar and coconut. The tin went into the oven for thirty minutes until the meringue was a pale brown.

While the slice cooked she cleaned down her station and began the pastry for individual apple pies. Maddie made apple pies every day following Gran's special recipe, and the customers loved them. Leaving the pastry to rest, it was time for the slice to come out of the oven to cool before cutting.

There was no idle time, as she had to grease all the pans for the pies. Fortunately, the filling had been made yesterday in bulk and they wouldn't take long to assemble, but first she had to cut her slice before it stuck to the pan. Oblivious to the rest of the kitchen, she slipped her knife around the outside edge, cleaned it, and cut along the length and then the width. Carefully lifting each rectangle she placed them on a clean tray ready for the display cabinet. Taking a step back she wiped her hands on her apron and admired her handiwork.

Uncle Roberto peered over her shoulder. "Very even. Good work, Maddie."

"Thank you." She smiled. Praise wasn't frequent from the eldest brother, so she knew when it came that her work was indeed good.

Oddly, he didn't leave and started moving from side to side like a polar bear. This wasn't a good sign. Usually when he was uncomfortable, he had bad news. Her stomach clenched. She couldn't afford to stay in the city if she lost her job. Besides, hadn't he just praised her? Still, her voice wobbled. "Did I do something wrong?"

He was a very large man. Not so much tall as round, and when he shook his head as he was doing, an extra chin wobbled. Leaning closer he almost whispered, except that would have been a waste of time, because the machines currently at work would drown out any ability to hear him.

"We are very happy with your work. This week you get a raise."

"A raise?" Maddie hadn't expected this, and it took a moment to sink in. "Thank you so much," she finally gushed.

He glanced around the kitchen and put a finger to his lips. "Do not tell the others."

She nodded several times to reassure him, and he lifted a large hand to pat her shoulder, which was more of a slap. It pushed her forward and automatically her hand reached out to steady herself—just missing the slices! Luck was on her side today, and she felt a rush of euphoria.

She couldn't wait to tell her boyfriend about the raise. The minute she thought this, the euphoria drained away and her stomach dipped once more. A raise was a good thing and something to be proud of, but Dalton wasn't impressed when she switched careers to work in the bakery. As a financial advisor she was paid very well and starting at the bottom of a bakery couldn't compare—something he reminded her of frequently. A high-powered advertising manager, Dalton also thought working in a bakery was a complete waste of her degree and told Maddie she was going backward. To be fair, last time she'd been home to Maple Falls a lot of people gave the impression that they agreed. It was hard not to be hurt over whispered opinions and snide remarks and harder still when those same opinions came from her partner.

Apart from her joy at doing what she loved, what made it easier to forge ahead came when she told Gran her plans. There were no recriminations, only encouragement.

"It's no one's business but yours, sweetheart. The people who care about you know you've been unhappy, and they only want what's best for you in the future, so pay the busybodies and trouble-makers no mind."

Naturally, Gran had been right. After one day at the bakery, even exhausted beyond her wildest imagination, she was so much happier. Without the shadow of a doubt, she knew she'd done the right thing. She smiled at the memory.

Maybe, for once, Dalton wouldn't sneer about her job and be happy for her.

CHAPTER TWO

Finishing work mid-afternoon, Maddie needed groceries if she was going to cook a meal and stopped by the Duane Reade on the corner before reaching home. As a treat she picked up a bunch of daffodils to brighten the apartment. When she found time, painting the dreary beige walls was a must.

After living in a large farmhouse her entire life, surrounded by large and rustic furniture, she hadn't grown accustomed to her current space. By comparison the one-bedroom apartment often felt claustrophobic, and, despite much smaller furniture, she constantly bumped into things. Her feet slowed on the stairs leading to the first-floor apartment, and Maddie took a deep breath as she unlocked the door, unsure whether Dalton would be there and wishing that didn't make her anxious.

"You're late." He sat on the sofa and shot a disapproving glance over his laptop.

She cringed at his accusing tone, opting not to make a fuss and ruin her good news. "I assumed you'd be here for dinner, so I stopped for groceries."

He crossed his legs on the coffee table, a sight Gran would have a fit over, and made no move to help with the bags. Big Red padded across the room and curled around her legs, forgiving her for leaving him all day much sooner than he usually did. She noted that he also stayed as far away from Dalton as possible. They did not get along and barely tolerated each other, which didn't make for a comfortable atmosphere most of the time.

Scratching the ginger head lovingly, she cooed, "Hello, boy. How was your day?"

"Charming," Dalton sneered. "What about me?"

She dumped the bags on the counter, noting he omitted to ask her about her day. "Did you have a good day, Dalton?"

He missed the dripping sarcasm. "No, I darn well didn't! I was frustrated like you wouldn't believe with the client from hell who ignored all my advice and wouldn't know a good deal if it bit him."

"That's a shame," she said before he could get into a monologue about a stranger's faults. "I had the perfect day at the bakery and some wonderful news." She waited a couple of heartbeats, but no question was forthcoming. "I got a raise."

Dalton rolled his eyes. "I imagine that brings you to minimum, right?"

Her heart sunk a little more. "I'm paid appropriately for an intern. Couldn't you be a little happy for me?"

"I would think that earning what you did in your last job should have made you happy enough for both of us."

Arrgh! Why did it always come down to money with him? "You know I hated my job."

He gave her an incredulous look. "What does that have to do with anything?"

The curtain in her mind, which had been gradually disintegrating, peeled away from the idea of him, and finally

Maddie admitted to herself how shallow Dalton had become. Maybe he'd always been this way. Her fingers tapped her thighs in an anxiety-release method her Grandad taught her after her mom left them and she'd been distraught. It wasn't working, but enough was enough. "If you think so little of my happiness, you should leave."

He blinked, then chuckled in disbelief. "Sheesh, where's your sense of humor? I was joking."

She crossed her arms. This line was often used as justification for upsetting her. "It didn't sound like it."

Dalton jumped up and came across the room wearing his most charming expression and opened his arms. "Babe, you need to lighten up a little. Where's my happy baker gone? You always make me smile, and I need that today." He hugged her tightly and kissed her forehead. "Sorry I wasn't more excited for you, but you know I love you. I guess I'm hungry, and you know how I get."

He rarely apologized. Was she being too harsh? When he was like this, she could forgive him for his weird sense of humor, which often seemed unkind. She leaned into him, enjoying the comfort. "You mean 'hangry'?"

He laughed again. "That's exactly right."

Laughter changed him from nice-looking to handsome, and she thawed a little more. "Okay, you can stay."

He released her and gave a mock bow. "Thank you, milady."

Maddie washed up in the bathroom and removed the tie from her long blonde braid. She brushed her hair for a minute or two, enjoying the soothing action. Dalton was only her second boyfriend and the first as a working adult. The fear that he was just as manipulative as the long-term one she'd had as a teenager crawled over her more often these days, which said more about her than it did them.

She'd never said she loved Dalton and lately had concerns

that she didn't always like him. That couldn't be a good thing in a relationship. Sometimes he stayed over, but tonight having spoiled the thrill of her pay increase, she was too tired and still too hurt to deal with him. Even if he was starving, she couldn't cook until she cleared her head.

By THE TIME she came back into the open plan room, he was glued to his laptop again. Big Red waited at the door, glaring at Dalton. If he ever laid a finger on her cat, they would definitely be over. Plucking her coat and scarf from the rack, she opened the door. "I'm taking Big Red for a walk. I'll cook dinner when I get back."

"Hmmm," was the only response.

As she closed the door, a loud bang reverberated from the floor above and was followed by the sound of scraping on the floor. Maddie peered up the stairwell while Big Red ran to investigate. They stood quietly, but there were no sounds of distress, only silence. Big Red's tail twitched, and she had that feeling again, but it seemed out of order to check up on her neighbor over moving furniture. "Come here, boy. Everything's fine."

The cat stared at the door and back a couple of times.

"What is it?"

"Meow."

"Well, that's not really enough to go on." Maddie tapped her thigh. "Let's leave Ms. Black alone and get your walk in before it grows too dark to see."

Winter nights fell early in New York, and reluctantly Big Red followed her. He loved a walk, although he was hardly housebound since she had the dog door installed in the window by the fire escape. She chuckled as she remembered him trying to get through the previous cat door. Maine coons were the biggest domestic cats, and Big Red was particularly large.

On the ground floor she pushed open the outer door in the foyer for him to saunter ahead down the concrete steps. Following, Maddie ran smack into one of the local beat officers who was also a regular customer at the bakery. He grabbed her by her forearms to steady her and smiled as Big Red wound around their legs.

"Where's the fire?"

"Sorry. I was watching Big Red instead of where I was going."

He smirked. "Taking the lion for a walk?"

Now this sort of teasing was what Maddie was used to and she grinned. "Yes, we're a little late today, and he's tired of being cooped up."

Officer Cameron snorted. "Is that what he tells you?"

"What do you mean?"

"He's been running around the fire escapes again."

This wasn't the first time she'd been informed of Big Red's activities when she wasn't around. "Oh, dear. Are people complaining?"

"One or two." He frowned. "Most people find him amusing, but if that cat keeps getting out, you're going to lose him."

Maddie hadn't considered that happening for months and shivered at the idea of Big Red being stolen, or worse. "I'll try to keep him closer to home when I'm there, only he's used to freedom, and I can't bear to shut him up completely."

"A lion does need space, but keeping a closer eye on him would be best."

She appreciated he was thinking of Big Red's safety, and not for the first time, Maddie experienced guilt about bringing Big Red to live in a city where there were far more dangers than he was used to, and where not everyone was as tolerant as Officer Cameron. At the time of her move, leaving Big Red at home in Maple Falls was an option it turned out she couldn't take. They'd been together since her high school days and were inseparable after her time at college, which had taken a toll on them. That alone made the decision to bring him to Manhattan easier, but it came at a price. Though he went out when he felt like it, he no longer roamed for miles like he had back home.

"Your hair looks nice like that."

Officer Cameron's words surprised her, and his cheeks pinked as soon as they were out.

"Thank you. I forgot my hat, so it's going to get messy really quick."

They stood awkwardly for a moment until Big Red meowed loudly. With an arched back his hair stood in all directions. At the same moment, Maddie heard a noise above them, which made her look up. Heart racing, she threw herself at Officer Cameron, and they landed in a heap on the stoop of the apartment block.

The officer flailed beneath her—as a body landed where they had just been standing.

CHAPTER THREE

Maddie's face was tucked under an armpit that wasn't hers, and she pushed the limb away to spit out a lump of hair before clambering off the shocked officer. Her hand shook as she helped him up while he continued to stare at her, the body, Big Red, and back to Maddie. Apparently, shock could be debilitating even for an officer of the law, so she took the initiative to check on the body, which hadn't so much as twitched.

Lifeless eyes stared up at the darkening sky and the snow turned pink in two small spots.

"It's Cleo Black," Maddie said sadly while searching for a pulse. "She's dead."

Officer Cameron gulped and knelt beside her. "Y-y-you saved me."

About to brush off his statement, she realized he was probably right. A body falling from that height would sure have an impact. "Lucky my reflexes kicked in at the right time after Big Red alerted me. You should call this in," she reminded him gently and glanced above them at the open window where a ripped curtain billowed in and out with the wind.

He nodded, his eyes still a little unfocused.

"Would you like me to do it, Adrian?"

The use of his Christian name made him register that he had a job to do, and he shook his head stiffly before making the call on the radio attached to his upper arm. When he was done, he seemed a little more centered and took off his coat to place over the twisted body, covering Cleo's face.

Maddie's grandad had trained her in thinking about more than the obvious, and made a couple of observations she recalled from prior to Cleo's unexpected arrival. "There were some funny noises coming from her apartment just now. Do you think you should go check it out?"

Officer Cameron blinked. "She lives on the third floor?"

"Yes. Right above me. I'm pretty sure she lives there alone."

He shivered, but a determined look came into his eyes. "What did the noise sound like?"

She tilted her head and closed her eyes to conjure up the sound, nodding at the memory. "Scraping across the floor. Preceded by a loud bang."

"That's it? No voices?"

She opened her eyes and frowned. "Not that I recall."

A siren sounded close by, and soon a police car pulled up followed by an ambulance. A tall, serious-looking man in a dark suit pushed his way through the gathering crowd. He glanced at the body and subjected Officer Cameron to a barrage of questions. The detective wasn't impressed that he hadn't gone to the apartment yet and dispatched an officer to the third floor immediately.

"Go ahead and rope off this area," he told Officer Cameron coolly. Finally he turned to Maddie who stood to the side of the steps with Big Red. "Ms. Flynn? I'm Detective

Bryant. I believe you were the only other witness along with Officer Cameron to the deceased's fall."

"I think so. There were people on both sides of the street, but they weren't close and didn't seem to notice right away."

"And how would you know that?" he asked suspiciously.

"As soon as I got off the officer, I looked around us and no one faced this way or came to see what happened, until Officer Cameron…ah…he made a noise."

Nonplussed, the detective pulled a notebook and pen from one of his shirt pockets. "Can you talk me through exactly what happened, please."

"I was walking my cat and bumped into your officer. Suddenly, Big Red warned me that something was wrong, and then there was a sound above us. I looked up to see the body hurtling down, and with seconds to spare I pushed Officer Cameron backward by leaping toward him. We landed on the steps and Ms. Black fell to where you see her. We touched nothing except for her wrist and throat to check for a pulse."

He studied her for several moments. "That is a very detailed account. Do you have training in crime scenes?"

"Not really. My grandad was ex-army, and he taught me to notice things."

"Hmmm. The officer said you also heard noises above your apartment."

"Technically I was in the stairwell when I heard the scraping and a bang, but her apartment is above mine. As I told Officer Cameron, that's all I heard prior to coming outside."

"And you were alone at the time?"

"I was with my cat, and he heard it too. Although, my boyfriend was inside my apartment, so he might have heard something more."

17

He gave her a strange look as he put the notebook away. "Let's go find out."

He opened the entryway door and nodded for her to precede him. Along the way, they could hear people talking, and the voices got louder as they approached Maddie's door on the second floor. They both looked up, and the detective seemed as anxious as she was to find out what had happened in that apartment.

"I suppose the fact no one came to tell you, or there wasn't any gunfire, means you can assume whoever did this is gone?"

He stiffened, looking down at her from his over-six-foot height. "We're not in the business of assuming, Ms. Flynn."

Still, he didn't deny it and after another glance upstairs pointed to the floor in front of him.

"Please wait here a moment." With that, he took a few giant strides, missing several steps, and disappeared inside Cleo Black's door.

Fingers tapping on her thighs, she debated whether to go inside her apartment. "Do you think he doesn't want me to speak to Dalton without him?" She spoke quietly, and Big Red seemed to nod. "It would make sense, since he doesn't know us and whether we might have answers to who did this or why."

Big Red ran up the stairs and sniffed at the door, then scampered back down to sit innocently at her side just as the detective came out.

The detective nodded as if reassured she hadn't budged and removed a pair of gloves before joining them on the landing. "Inside, please."

The command was a little icy. What, if anything, had he found? Her mind raced. And who might it incriminate?

CHAPTER FOUR

Once again, Dalton didn't bother to look up at Maddie's arrival. "That was a long walk, and I'm still starving. Will dinner be long?"

His querulous voice embarrassed her, and she coughed nervously. "There's been an accident."

That made him look up and notice they had a visitor. He frowned at the detective beside her. "What did you do now, and who the heck is this?"

"What?" Her voice rose in amazement at the accusation and that he hadn't thought to ask if she was okay or what the accident could be.

The detective moved further into the room. "I'm Detective Bryant. Why would you assume your girlfriend had done something?"

Dalton sat up straighter at the question, or perhaps it was the detective's tone, which was anything but friendly. Considering what had recently happened he could be excused for that, but he didn't look impressed by her boyfriend's attitude, and neither was she.

Licking his lips, Dalton sighed dramatically. "She's always

sticking her nose into people's business is what I mean. Picking up stray animals and kids wherever she goes or stopping to talk to homeless people, she never thinks of the consequences."

Maddie blinked as his words cut into her. Why would he say such a thing in front of the detective? Did he want to incriminate her over something he had no clue about. "If making sure people are okay is considered being nosy, then I guess I must be." The words forced through gritted teeth finally drew his attention to her displeasure.

"You know what I mean, babe."

"I'm not sure that I do—babe."

"Okay, well, let's not make a fuss right now." Dalton gave the detective a look that could have only been more offensive if he'd rolled his eyes.

"Fuss? A woman is dead." Her voice rose at least two octaves.

The detective, who had been studying the interchange with interest, chose that moment to intervene. "You might like to know that your girlfriend just saved an officer's life."

"Maddie?" Dalton scoffed.

She stormed into the kitchen and put water to boil. It had been cold outside, and coffee would be welcome, but this was really to divert herself. Hot enough under the collar at Dalton's dismissal of her acts of kindness, which cost him nothing, and the earlier indication that she served no purpose other than to cook his meals, Maddie had the uncommon urge to screech at him like a banshee. A woman was dead. She'd seen her plummet to the ground. Surely that required a little bit of commiseration and compassion for witnessing that and the life lost.

The detective beckoned her. "Please take a seat, Ms. Flynn. I have a few more questions."

Dalton smirked, and Maddie took a kitchen chair so she

didn't have to sit beside him. The detective took the other one. He glanced at each of them and cleared his throat. Maddie was still embarrassed, and anger pressed on her chest like a heavy blanket.

"Ms. Flynn saw Ms. Black fall from her apartment, which I believe is above us. Did you hear anything, Mr...?"

Dalton stiffened, his face turning a strange, mottled color. "Dalton Aker. Are you sure she fell from that floor? I didn't hear anything odd, but I was working." He nodded at the laptop, oblivious to the fact that he hadn't so much as stood when the detective arrived and was only now introducing himself because he had no choice.

The detective had probably dealt with this level of ignorance before, and he simply continued. "No scraping along the floor?" He looked up at the ceiling and while words couldn't be made out there was the sound of muffled voices.

"I repeat, I heard nothing," Dalton said adamantly. He grew paler when he glanced to the window beyond them. "You're saying she fell from out of a window, down past this one, almost landed on Maddie, and now the woman is dead?"

Despite it being the truth, Maddie didn't appreciate his phrasing. Before she could react, footsteps sounded on the stairs outside the apartment, and she looked toward the door, but whoever it was kept going downstairs.

"That's right." Detective Bryant pointed to the ceiling. "An officer is checking Ms. Black's apartment as we speak."

"Sounds like a few officers. At least they're doing something to find out what happened, I guess. Although the press is going to have a field day once they find out about this, if they haven't already." Dalton suddenly grimaced distastefully. "Was it suicide?"

It would be a fair assumption that Dalton, and not the gravity of the situation, had the detective looking less patient by the minute.

"We have no way of knowing until we've investigated things."

"Wait a minute." Dalton leaned forward. "You think she was pushed, don't you?"

"As I said, we are investigating the incident and don't have all the details yet." The detective tapped the pad with his pen. "Now, what can you tell me about Ms. Black?"

Dalton shrugged. "She kept to herself. I hardly saw her."

Maddie's jaw dropped.

"And you, Ms. Flynn? You seem surprised by Mr. Aker's answer."

"Dalton doesn't live here," she spoke flatly. "It would surprise me if he had any knowledge of anyone else in the building."

The detective raised an eyebrow and gave Dalton and Maddie another searching glance before indicating with his pen for her to continue.

"What I meant was, Dalton rarely sees any of the residents. However, I can tell you that Ms. Black was always courteous and said 'hi' when I passed her on the stairs. She hardly made any noise before last night."

"Thank goodness," Dalton added. "These old buildings are hardly soundproof."

"How long has she lived here?"

Maddie frowned as she thought of the first time she'd met Cleo. "Maybe two months."

"Do you know who lived in the apartment before her?"

"It was a couple, and they were here longer than me. They moved back to Ohio as they were starting a family and didn't want to bring up a child in an apartment."

Dalton snorted. "See, what did I tell you about her."

Maddie glared at him. "There is nothing wrong with sharing pleasantries and good news."

"People should keep their private lives just that, private," he scoffed.

The detective made a sound of disapproval. "You said there wasn't much noise before last night."

"That's right. I thought I heard Cleo arguing with someone, but I can't be sure."

Detective Bryant jotted something down then stood. "I'm going to check on things upstairs, but I could be back with more questions."

"Tonight?" Dalton seemed uneasy.

The detective frowned. "Is that a problem?"

"We were about to eat."

"Dalton!" Maddie exclaimed in horror. "There's been a death."

"We still have to eat," he said plaintively.

Disgusted by his casual attitude, she shook her head while the detective took Dalton's details, then she saw him out. "I'll be here all night, Detective, but do you want to take my details now and get that out the way?"

"Officer Cameron already gave them to me." The detective glanced at Dalton, whose feet were back on the coffee table, his laptop propped up in front of him on a cushion. A flicker of annoyance ran across the stern features and was gone in an instant. "If I don't get back tonight, and you are going to be alone later, it would pay to deadbolt this door, Ms. Flynn."

The way he said this, rather than the words, made Maddie gulp. She was reasonably sure she wasn't imagining things. Cleo's demise after all those noises was suspicious, and the detective clearly thought so too.

"Thank you. I will."

He again took the stairs two at a time, and when he'd gone inside Maddie came back into the room and leaned against the door with a heavy sigh.

"Did you have to flirt with him?"

She swung around to face Dalton, almost at the end of her rope. "Pardon?"

"I'll be here all night," Dalton said in a simpering voice.

"Stop being a fool. This is serious."

"You know what?" He packed away his laptop and pulled the strap over his shoulder. "Forget dinner. I can't deal with all this drama. Whether the woman killed herself or not, what possible help could I be? I certainly didn't do anything to cause it." He strode to the door. "I might give you a call tomorrow and see if this has blown over."

She waited until he was outside. "Don't bother calling tomorrow, and thanks so much for your support." With that she slammed and locked the door and not just because the detective said to. Dalton might want to comment on her sarcasm or in another universe apologize, but there was no way he was getting back in here regardless of any unlikely change of heart.

"How did I put up with him for so long?" she groaned to the world at large.

Big Red jumped onto the back of the sofa and meowed loudly several times.

"Yes. I know you told me he wasn't right for us. You must admit that in the beginning he had some good qualities."

The cat glared at her, and she managed a shaky laugh. "Okay, maybe I had blinders on, and you were right all along."

Once she'd flopped onto the sofa, Big Red jumped up and snuggled next to her. Maybe he thought the admittance was worth a hug.

"I'm thinking that all we need from now on is each other. What do you say, buddy?"

The cat head butted her gently, purring loudly.

"Deal. Just us. Although, you might have to help me

explain the situation to Dalton. He has this habit of never listening to me."

Big Red suddenly licked at the fur on his paws, and Maddie couldn't help but imagine he was momentarily flashing his claws for effect.

Maddie put her hand over them, and they slid away. "We'll bring them out if needed," she promised.

CHAPTER FIVE

D uring the night, Maddie heard a few noises. She toyed with the idea of ringing the police, but the sounds weren't coming from exactly above, and there were other apartments to the side and below her. Besides, Big Red seemed unfazed, so she put it down to imagination just to get some sleep.

It was easier to dismiss as she bustled about getting ready, but she did check the stairwell before cautiously making her way outside and on to the bakery. It wasn't that she expected the murderer to jump out at her but the person was still out there somewhere and Maddie's nerves prickled at the thought.

She stopped about halfway to send Big Red home. Worried that he might get lost or run over, and mindful of Officer Cameron's comment, it was the right thing to do, but she immediately missed his presence. He had an uncanny sense of danger, which was probably due to his keen sense of smell and hearing, she only knew that she trusted his instincts.

When Camille arrived at work, she hurried to Maddie's

station, eyes like saucers. "What's this I hear about a suicide in your building?"

"I don't think it was a suicide, but how did you find out so soon?"

"Are you kidding? My phone was ringing hot with the news as soon as I turned it on. How do you know it wasn't suicide?"

"I don't know for sure, but from the way he was handling things, the detective in charge didn't seem to think so," she admitted truthfully. A lengthy account ensued of her not knowing Ms. Black well and how she had seen her fall. The shock this sent around the kitchen was enough for everything to go quiet for a time, apart from the machines which ran pretty much all day.

"I'm sorry you had to see such a thing," Uncle Joey said gently.

"It was awful and I can't help wondering what happened to her before that and what led to that moment." Maddie was blessed or cursed, depending on how you looked at it, with a vivid imagination and it bothered her to think that the noises she'd heard earlier must be attributable to Cleo's death. If only she'd checked on her neighbor, this might have been avoided.

Thankfully, Uncle Roberto clapped his hands before she descended into despair. "Enough! Back to work and leave Maddie alone. She's had a terrible shock and cannot forget it for a second if you're badgering her for gory details. And, we have customers waiting on cannoli."

The others scampered away, and Uncle Roberto came to her not long afterward and asked if she would like to go home. This was a big deal in the bakery when usually an employee had to be on death's door to get time off.

She smiled gratefully. "I'd rather keep working and try to focus on something else." To a certain extent this was true, though Maddie couldn't seem to shut out any of it for more than a moment or two. There was also the fact that going home wasn't exactly appealing.

He nodded, his face lit with respect and he left her to bake, but over the course of the morning she often felt his and the rest of the staff's eyes on her.

A couple of hours later, as she was nursing a glass of water in the small lunchroom, Uncle Joey brought her a hot butter chicken pie.

"Your favorite, Maddie."

Unsure of her ability to eat anything, she appreciated his kindness. "Thank you, it looks delicious as always."

Camille placed a large coffee at her elbow and patted her shoulder. "You doing okay?"

"I'm fine. Just a little wobbly now and again."

"You're amazing. If that were me, I'd be a gibbering mess wrapped in a blanket on my bed. Speaking of which, do you want to come spend a few days with me? I still have a pull-out couch."

Camille's place was even smaller than Maddie's, and though it was tempting to not be alone right now, in her current state of mind she'd be poor company. "Thanks for the offer, but I want to do a little more practice before tomorrow. Plus, I need to get my chef's clothes ironed and packed."

Camille gaped for a moment. "I forgot you're leaving first thing in the morning. Will you be okay to go to the contest?"

"I think so." Maddie shrugged. "With my nerves focused on what happened I've hardly thought about cooking in a contest.."

"You're so brave, Maddie." Camille hugged her. "And the offer still stands when you get back. Unless you're going to stay at Dalton's."

Maddie choked on the coffee. "His flat mates are at war

29

again, so probably not." As much as she wanted to tell Camille that she wouldn't stay with Dalton for a million dollars and why, it was too much to go into right now. Especially after Cleo's death and his reaction to it. She hadn't liked it one bit and didn't know how to explain it to herself let alone someone else.

"I guess having him at your place will make you feel safer."

Camille's half smile was meant to be reassuring, only she didn't like Dalton any more than Big Red. Not that she'd admitted it to Maddie, but her face was an open book and so easy to read between the lines.

"Mmmm," she said non-commitedly. "You should come over Friday after work so we can have a girl's night in."

"Sounds great. I'll bring the popcorn and movie."

They would have plenty to talk about, and Maddie looked forward to sharing her news in a less emotional way than she might do now, if only to get it off her chest.

Naturally, everyone at work was discussing the murder, but after Uncle Roberto's interference, they were being careful not to do so that she could hear. With her mind playing the falling body on loop, this was a blessing. Although, the uncles seemed to be having earnest discussions, and she was convinced this was about the murder and how they could protect her. While they were exacting bosses, they had hearts of gold and looked after their employees with father-like devotion. It warmed her heart to feel included in this.

By the end of her shift, she was shattered, anxious to get home to Big Red and lock herself away in silence. At this rate and the way her nerves were frayed, she was unconvinced that she'd be up to the competition tomorrow.

"Good luck in the competition," Uncle Joey called across

the kitchen as she pushed her apron into the laundry bag by the back door. "And stay safe."

"Yes, make sure you lock up tight tonight and call one of us if there is any more trouble. And for tomorrow, keep calm the way you do here, and I know you'll do the bakery proud," Uncle Roberto added while Uncle Carlo nodded and frowned in the background.

This was high praise from Uncle Roberto, though it added to the pressure she'd been in denial about. Of course, that could be a good thing if it took her mind off the murder the way baking had earlier today. She hoped so. Another sleepless night wasn't something to aspire to.

When she was almost home, Big Red waited on the corner of the street, his head turned to the apartments. A figure darted out of the entranceway and disappeared in a sudden throng of pedestrians.

Her steps quickened as she tried to look over their heads, but she wasn't particularly tall, and whoever had been there was long gone. She would've put it down to fanciful thought if it weren't for Big Red sitting on a trash can doing the same thing.

With a sigh she opened the door for him and walked up the stairs with zero enthusiasm. When she looked up to her door Maddie got such a surprise that she stumbled. Someone sat on the top step.

CHAPTER SIX

B ig Red wrapped himself around the man's ankles, and Maddie began to breathe again.

Detective Bryant untangled himself and came down the steps. "Sorry I couldn't get back to you last night. I did stop by early this morning, but there was no one home."

"You'd have to be up early to catch me, Detective." She gave a wry smile. "I'm a baker and gone before 4 a.m."

He grimaced. "I thought I was a morning person, but that's a little too early. Is now a good time to talk?"

"Sure. Shall we go inside? It's a little cold out here." Locating the key in the bottom of her bag with less trouble than usual, Maddie involuntarily glanced up to the ceiling and shivered again, not entirely due to the cold landing. Squeezing past him, she opened the door without waiting for an answer.

The three of them went inside, where thankfully it was noticeably warmer. Big Red led the detective to the table while she put her bag on the counter of the kitchenette.

"Please take a seat. Can I make you coffee?"

"Only if you're having some."

"Definitely. After the walk home and the cold weather, it's what I look forward to most."

He sat and pulled out a notebook and pen from an inside pocket of his dark suit jacket. "Where is your bakery?"

Maddie was confused on two counts. "Did Officer Cameron not tell you? I don't own it. I'm an employee at Fournier's Bakery. Although, one day I'd like to have my own," she added wistfully. "My friend and I talk about owning one together all the time, but you have no idea how much the rents on suitable properties are."

He raised an eyebrow. "And the address of your current employment?"

"Oh, yes. I assumed Officer Cameron would have told you that as well." She gave it to him, a little embarrassed by her burbling. Why would he be interested in her long-term plans for the future?

"Thank you. I do have all your details, but I like to hear things firsthand. How well did you know Ms. Black?"

Was this how he decided if a person was being honest? Ask several questions and take note of how they were answered—grandad would approve. "As I said, we'd hardly spoken to each other. She was private, and I don't keep the most sociable hours. I'm up so early and in bed by 8 p.m. if possible. I like eight hours sleep." She'd done the over-sharing thing again and caught a small twitch at the corner of his mouth.

"One would hope that you take time for a little fun on the weekends?"

She shrugged and poured two mugs of strong coffee. "I work six days and I'm usually shattered by Saturday night. Sugar? Milk?"

"Black is perfect. How does Mr. Aker feel about the lack of a social life?"

Her hand stilled over the coffee pot for a moment. The

question didn't seem relevant to the case, yet he looked very business-like as she handed him the mug. "He's used to it and goes out on his own if I'm not up to it." She didn't add that he did this every weekend, and during the week most nights, because it would probably sound resentful. While this was certainly initially true, as time went by, she felt only relief not to have the pressure of agreeing to something she didn't want to do. This was embarrassing to admit—even to herself.

"I see. I caught up with Mr. Aker before I came here, and we discussed his whereabouts yesterday and how often he's here. Could you tell me your version of that?"

Maddie gaped for a moment. Did the detective suspect Dalton? And what did he mean by version? Detective Bryant watched her closely, and she shook herself. Whatever Dalton said she could only tell the truth as she knew it and wasn't about to lie for him. "He's here most evenings until I go to bed and occasionally stays over. Although, he hasn't for the last few weeks."

"He was here when you got home from work yesterday."

"That's right. We had a short conversation, then I left him here while I took Big Red for his walk."

His face lightened somewhat. "Are you serious about walking a cat?"

"He's more than a cat." She tilted her head, only mildly embarrassed by the admission, because she'd told this story to many disbelievers. "We're best friends and have been for years. I suppose I'm not technically taking him for a walk. He likes to walk with me, and we like each other's company, so it's a mutual arrangement."

"Hmmm. Your neighbor downstairs says the cat walks around the neighborhood when you're at work, which would imply that he doesn't actually require further exercise."

This was beginning to sound like an interrogation one might see on a TV spoof and the thought made her snort.

35

"While that's true, he still likes to go out with me because he gets lonely and likes to show me where he's been that day. It's a way to get some one-on-one time."

He smirked and then coughed to hide it. "So, Mr. Aker doesn't walk with you?"

She laughed. "No. He's a bit like you and sees it as unnecessary. Plus, they aren't exactly buddies."

He gave her a funny look she couldn't understand, and she blurted, "Although, they do tolerate each other."

"I see. Getting back to the crime, would you describe the noises from above once more, please."

She nodded, closing her eyes for a moment, which helped her to focus rather than see the way his looks were rapidly morphing into ones of pity. "There was a loud bang, then the sound of something scraping along the floor. It was all over in seconds."

"You didn't think to check on your neighbor?"

Maddie sighed. This exact question had bothered her all night. "In hindsight, I wish I had. Only Ms. Black kept to herself like most people around here. I didn't want to intrude, and there was honestly no sound of distress."

One eyebrow shot up. "You listened out for that?"

She nodded. "After the argument the night before, I thought I should. Big Red went up to her door to check and when there were no further sounds he didn't seem too perturbed, so we left for our walk. Naturally, I regret that now, but then again, if the murderer was inside, we could have been in danger."

The detective gave Big Red a speculative glance. "Most definitely. You could say that it was a better option to leave the building."

"Perhaps. I do feel guilty though."

His eyes narrowed again. "In what way?"

"If I had merely knocked and startled the killer, Ms. Black

might still be alive. I couldn't sleep last night for thinking about that."

"You should also consider that Ms. Black was already dead by then."

Maddie shivered. "So, it wasn't the fall that killed her? I did wonder after I saw her properly."

"I beg your pardon?"

"There was a dent on her temple." Maddie tapped her head to illustrate exactly where. "It was already beginning to bruise, though it looked recent. Possibly she got it on the way down. Since she landed on her back, the landing wouldn't have attributed to that."

The pen poised midair while he studied her for a moment. "That is a very interesting observation."

"It was a long enough night to think on all the facts. You know, they way her eyes were bulging and bloodshot. Plus, there was little blood. By the way, she didn't hit anything on the way down that I saw."

"It happened very fast. How can you be sure?"

"Three floors are not a long time to fall." She shrugged. "Maybe three Mississippis at most. When Big Red alerted me, I looked up instantly. A second later and Ms. Black would have landed on Officer Cameron and me."

He held his palm up. "Back up. You lost me at Mississippi?"

"It's a way to count seconds. You know. One Mississippi, two Mississippi, etc."

His mouth twitched. "You had time to count?"

"No. It wasn't meant to be literal. I just meant that in that second I jumped on your officer, Cleo Black could have barely been in the air for a few seconds."

He shook his head. "Okay. Do you recall whether she had any visitors?"

"Not one in all the time she lived here, but of course I'm not here most of the day."

He nodded. "And do you know what she did for a job?"

Maddie shrugged. "Like I said, she didn't invite conversation. Sorry, I'm not much help, am I?"

"I wouldn't say that." He stood. "Thanks for your time and the coffee. Don't forget, if you have any more epiphanies or remember something, give me a call anytime."

"Of course. I hope you find the person responsible soon."

He studied her for a moment. "You haven't considered moving out for a while? Perhaps staying with your boyfriend?"

"I don't think that would work." She grimaced, then coughed, hoping she hadn't inferred that a whole night or longer with Dalton right now wasn't an attractive proposition. It was true she didn't want the detective to think she was accusing Dalton of anything—except being a terrible boyfriend. "Actually, I won't be around tomorrow as I'm in a baking competition in Queens and won't be back until late."

"I can't promise to have a suspect by then."

"I know, but you might."

"I love your optimism." He smiled and with a last pat for Big Red left her with a lot to think about.

She blushed and couldn't understand why. Unless it was the fact that she hadn't been paid a compliment by anyone except her bosses in a very long time.

CHAPTER SEVEN

Another bad night's sleep, happily without any noises real or imagined, had Maddie struggling to function even though she didn't have to leave as early to get to the competition as she would have to be at the bakery. Cleo Black was still on her mind as she made coffee and dressed.

The tape across Cleo's door was another stark reminder of the murder above her, and that she might have heard the event happening.

Snow sprinkled down on the drive to the station, and Maddie shivered as she got out of the cab and went through the automatic doors, wheeling a small carry-on bag. Suddenly she was knocked sideways by a man in a hurry who didn't so much as glance her way. She stumbled into a woman who grabbed her to keep them both from falling.

"Whoa! Steady."

Maddie righted herself. "I'm so sorry."

"Don't apologize." The woman picked up her handbag from the floor. "I saw that guy barrel into you. People can be so rude."

"I guess he has a train to catch." Maddie gave a wry smile.

The woman laughed loudly. "Do you think? Lucky we all don't behave that way."

"Exactly. Thanks for catching me. I'm Madeline Flynn, but friends call me Maddie."

"No problem. I don't suppose an awkward forced hug in a crowded station counts as friendship, but pleased to meet you, Maddie. I'm Dani Moon."

"Close enough in my book." Maddie grinned. "Are you headed to Queens, Dani?"

"That's right. How did you know?"

"It's the next train from here in this direction, and that's where I'm going."

"How observant. Will we sit together? I always think a conversation makes the journey faster."

"Me too," Maddie agreed wholeheartedly.

"Only you don't want to be stuck talking with just anyone. I've had that happen, and then you get the reverse where you want to put your elbows in your ears."

Maddie laughed. "I don't think I'll have that problem. In fact, I think this will be the quickest trip ever."

"In that case we should get to the train before we're left behind."

In truth there was plenty of time. Maddie hated being late and always got where she needed to be ahead of schedule. Lucky for Maddie and her well-being, Dani was of the same mind. They ambled down the wide hall and out to the platform. A movement in the carriage beside them caught her eye—it was the rude man. She couldn't see his face, but the coat was the same, as was the hat pulled low over his eyes to shield most of his face along with a turned-up collar.

While Maddie pondered whether a coat worn that way on a full train wouldn't be hot and potentially claustrophobic, Dani waxed lyrical about her work as an assistant to a producer.

"The show is one we do each year and often in other cities. The contestants are so eager my heart breaks for the non-winners. I say it like that because while there's only one winner, the others are all winners as far as I'm concerned. How brave must they be to put themselves out there to be judged?"

Maddie stopped in her tracks. "By any chance is this a cooking competition you're working on?"

"That's right. Why?"

"It might be the one I'm entered into."

"No way! *Queen or King of the Kitchen?*"

"Yes, that's it! How coincidental that we've met like this. I must admit I'm nervous."

Dani's lips pursed. "You don't look it."

"We're not there yet, so there's plenty of time for that to escalate." Maddie laughed. "Shall we find our seats?" She carried only the wheeled tote bag and her handbag, a large affair that held her laptop as well as purse, keys, and various paraphernalia. It was getting a little ratty and was a source of amusement to all her friends who liked nice luggage, but she held onto it as if it were made of gold while they walked through the train.

Dani was oddly quiet and stopped by their seats with a serious look on her pretty oval face. "I have to tell you that I can't help you today in any way. If that was your plan by us 'accidentally meeting', you should know I have no sway over the producer or judges."

Maddie's eyes widened in horror. "It honestly never crossed my mind."

Dani shrugged. "I want to believe you, but it seems odd that you bump into me and next minute we're buddies."

Maddie's heart hammered at the accusation. "I'm not a big believer in coincidences either, however, I can assure you that this was not a pre-meditated meeting. You saw that man knock me flying, and I'm grateful to you for ensuring I didn't hurt myself, but if you can't accept what I'm saying I'm sure I can swap seats."

Dani studied her for a few seconds then waved at the seat next to her. "Never mind. Let's sit down. You seem like an upfront person, and I'm being melodramatic."

The train was already filling quickly, and feeling awkward Maddie did sit next to Dani. She was also a little annoyed until she gave it more thought. While she'd done nothing wrong, Dani had been very upset. "Does that happen often to you?"

"People latching onto me?" Dani grimaced. "More than I like, but usually at the venue once the contestants work out who to target. There I go again with the dramatics," she scoffed. "It's not all or even most of them. I should have said there's usually a couple at each show who think I'm their golden ticket."

"That's horrible. No wonder you're wary of accidental meetings."

Dani acknowledged this with a faint smile. "Sometimes it's not pleasant, but mostly they're just trying to get a little assistance with the right and wrong way to go about things in relation to interacting with the judges. I don't blame them for that. It's the ones who pretend to like and know me, then ask me to help them as if they deserve it. That's hard to swallow."

Maddie's heart tugged at her chest. "And yet you befriended me right away."

"What can I say?" Dani shrugged. "I'm a friendly girl who gets less friendly the closer I get to work."

"It makes perfect sense when you explain it that way. I'm sorry you have to deal with people who want to use you. Here's a thought, why don't we talk about other things?"

Dani tilted her head. "Things like men?"

"No, thank you." Maddie shook her head firmly.

"Ahh. I detect troubles in that sphere?"

Maddie clutched the handle on her bag and stuck it further between her black-trousered knees. She was a private person, but the urge to confide in someone was tempting, and she wouldn't see Camille until tomorrow. "I decided last night to finish with my boyfriend."

"Bleh! That's the hardest part—making the decision. The next is telling them when they have no clue. Unless he knows that it isn't working?"

Maddie frowned. "I have absolutely no idea if he realizes it or not. We argue all the time but never actually discuss anything. It drives me crazy that he won't listen when I want to discuss our relationship."

"That's a deal breaker if ever I heard one." Dani blushed. "Sorry, it's none of my business."

"No need to apologize—I agree. I wish I'd had the sense to end it sooner, but he can be incredibly charming when he chooses. He swept me off my feet with lovely words, flowers, and gifts. Flowers die and chocolates don't last. Now I see him for who he really is, and I don't like it."

Dani nodded sagely. "While chocolates combined with good looks are tempting, you can't sustain being false forever. There have been a couple of schmucks in my past, and I like to think I've learned something from each of them. Still, if a guy pretends to be something other than what he is, and does it well, then how can you know not to touch him with a ten-foot pole?"

"In other words, there's a lot to be said for being single," Maddie added.

"True, although not forever. Just long enough to put yourself back together and remember who you are, and that whether you have a boyfriend or not doesn't have to define you."

Maddie chuckled. "You're very wise. I wish I'd met you some time ago."

Dani winked. "My girlfriends call it being smug, because my latest man is so cute, and I can still be myself around him."

"You'll have to give me the recipe for one of those."

"In my humble opinion, it's ten percent caution and ninety percent luck."

By the time they got to their station, Maddie hadn't laughed so much in ages and told Dani so.

"That's me, good for a laugh. Now, the venue isn't far away, so I'll walk with you to the corner of the building before we have to part ways. If my boss sees me hanging out with a contestant she'll give me a lecture, and I don't care to ruin the day so early."

"I understand completely. Thanks for keeping me company. It helped keep my mind off the competition and other things."

"I'm glad."

They joined the throng of travelers moving out into the hustle and bustle of a large city. The snow had stopped, and as they neared the crosswalk Dani leaned toward her.

"I'll leave you here. Good luck and maybe I'll see you on the way home. Or are you staying in Queens?"

"I toyed with the idea, since we finish late, but I have a cat at home I'd rather get back to. He isn't happy about me being away for too long."

Dani nudged her. "Are you sure you're talking about a cat?"

"He is a very special cat," Maddie chuckled.

"He must be. Anyway, I want to get home to my new man, so I'll keep an eye out for you at the station."

Maddie waved as they separated and made her way into the event center. Showing her pass, she was directed through the roped-off areas to the kitchens. They were set up in four rows with three in each.

Each kitchen had a bench with hobs and a sink. Underneath was an oven, with shelves on either side holding all the utensils and pans required. Every counter held a large mixer and a wooden box. Fridges and freezers lined a wall at the side of the room to be used for setting ingredients.

Everything she saw reminded Maddie of the shows she had watched with Gran since she was small, and still did when she had time. Now here she was about to compete in one. This wasn't one of the bigger shows, but it would be aired, and a stepping stone to them. It was thrilling as well as nerve-wracking, and she couldn't wait to start.

She was the first contestant to arrive and found her area before being greeted by a stage hand who directed her to a waiting room and the place to sign in. There was a water station, a table with croissants, bagels, meats, cheeses, spreads, and more importantly, a large coffee pot.

There'd been no time for breakfast or to finish her coffee at home, but she hadn't been hungry, which wasn't unusual when she always got up so early. There was a sign that said to help herself. She poured coffee and took a croissant.

She managed one bite of the flaky pastry which was almost on a par with the ones from the bakery just as the others began to arrive. They looked just as nervous, apart from one man who eyed the rest of them with a sniff and waited impatiently to get to the coffee. She smiled at everyone, and they introduced themselves except for Mr. Haughty, who avoided all eye contact.

"Hi, I'm Maddie," she said to a young woman who was leaning against the wall, wringing her hands and gulping.

"Louise. Do you know where the bathroom is?" she asked desperately.

"Are you unwell?"

The woman nodded, growing paler by the second.

"I'll find it. Wait here." She placed her plate and coffee on the table and ran to the door. Spying Dani across the stage Maddie waved at her and her new friend came toward her warily. "I don't have time to chat, and it wouldn't be a good look if I did."

Maddie shook her head. "I'm not here for a chat. You have a contestant that I'm pretty sure is about to be sick, and we have no idea where the bathrooms are."

Immediately contrite, Dani pointed behind the green room. "You have to go around the corner there. I'm sorry, I meant to leave instructions." She hesitated and looked over her shoulder where a smartly dressed woman was issuing orders.

Maddie could see Dani was busy and feeling the pressure. "That's okay, I'll take her."

"Would you mind?" Dani asked hopefully.

"Not at all." Maddie raced back to Louise and managed to get her to the bathroom just in time for the woman to be violently ill in private.

A few minutes later, Louise came out wiping her face with a damp handkerchief. "Thank you, Maddie," she said shyly. "I'm so embarrassed."

"There's no need to be." Maddie waved the apology away. "I'm the only one who knows, and I won't say a word."

Louise smiled gratefully. "I guess we should get back."

They returned to the room to find that everyone was now on stage. As they joined the group, the producer gave them a stern glance before explaining the way the contest would run and that they had a timeframe to adhere to.

"I guess we should consider ourselves told off," Maddie said out of the corner of her mouth and was pleased to hear Louise give a small giggle.

"Also, due to the ill health of Ricardo Varden, we have a change of judge."

There were some nervous mutterings and the producer stilled them with a rap on her clipboard.

"As I mentioned, Ricardo isn't well, but he insisted the show go on, so he called in a favor. I don't think any of you will be disappointed with his replacement," she said with pride. "My assistant will direct you to your stations."

Dani showed them to their areas and in a stroke of luck Maddie found Louise positioned next to her. It felt good to have a friendly face nearby, and she gave her neighbor a thumbs up as the judge arrived.

Most of the contestants gasped as she did at the new judge. It was such a massive shock that she could barely accept this was happening to her.

Celebrity chef Lyra St. Claire waved to them before taking her place in the middle of the stage. She was gorgeous with a mane of thick red hair that ran in waves down her back. Dressed in green with a cinched-in waist, she had the figure of Nigella Lawson, and cooked with the same passion.

In a short span of time, she had become an icon and then an entrepreneur. Not only was she a judge for cooking contests across the country, but Lyra also had her own show where she interviewed celebrities who liked to cook, as well as opening a fancy restaurant in L.A. called La Joliesse. Although she was touted as being a home cook, there was nothing plain about Lyra St. Claire's food. Maddie loved to try out her recipes whenever she could—and like a dream, here was Lyra in the flesh about to try Maddie's cooking.

Maddie assumed the judge would be aloof and critical. Yet, here was arguably the most famous chef in the country walking among them, chatting with the contestants and putting them at ease. It was inspiring, and she hoped this would help relax the still-pale Louise.

Just then, the smug contestant left his area to stand in front of Lyra. The merest glance of annoyance crossed her smiling face before she turned away from him and moved on.

Her personal assistant, Maggie, blocked him from following. "Mr. Thomas, please return to your station. Ms. St Claire will be by to see you in good time."

He glared at her, but the assistant had probably seen this a hundred times and merely raised an eyebrow as if daring him to argue. After the briefest hesitation, he huffed and moved back as instructed.

There was something familiar about him, but what? Had he come into the bakery and been rude to her? Maddie took a deep breath. This was no time to let her mind wander.

If she wanted to impress the judges, she had to focus.

CHAPTER EIGHT

Maggie Parker was making the introductions, and when she got to Maddie she glanced at a clipboard briefly before nodding encouragingly at her. "Madeline Flynn, originally from Maple Falls, works in a Manhattan bakery."

The great Lyra St. Claire smiled at Maddie. "Oh, yes. Your bio sounded so familiar. Did you know that I come from Fairview?"

"I read that." Maddie nodded enthusiastically. Actually, she'd read everything written about Lyra St. Claire and loved that they had a small town in common. It meant anyone was capable of the same heady heights as Lyra had reached. "It's a very pretty town and not far from Maple Falls as the crow flies."

"Practically neighbors." Lyra chuckled. "Small towns are great, but like me you obviously had to go somewhere larger to learn more."

"It was a series of events that led me here, but you are the main inspiration for me becoming a baker, along with my

Gran who is a fantastic cook. I mean, she's almost as good as you." Maddie blushed furiously, but Lyra merely laughed.

"My mom's a pretty handy cook too, which helped instill the desire in me to bake and also to do it well."

"I think they go hand in hand. Although I've often thought that loving how something tastes is great, having a passion for making it repeatedly while improving a recipe is even more important."

Lyra grinned. "It sounds like we have a lot in common. I hope you cook as well as you express yourself. Good luck."

Maddie blushed again, wondering at her nerve and when she would learn to keep some things inside her head and not blurt out every little thing. "Thank you," she called after the chef, but Lyra was now at Louise's station, and Maddie heaved a sigh, wondering if she'd just reached groupie status.

"You did fine," Lyra's assistant whispered and moved on as if she hadn't said a thing.

Maggie Parker knew Lyra better than anyone, and Maddie's heart swelled. If the assistant thought she hadn't been an idiot, then maybe she still had a shot at being taken seriously. She had better deliver a good dish to prove she had the necessary skills to be here.

Imposter syndrome ran riot as she watched Lyra chat to each contestant. When the chef got to Austin Thomas's station, she was still smiling, but something in the tilt of her chin made Maddie think she wasn't the only one who thought this guy was trouble.

From two rows away she could hear the man talking himself up. Not that she had an issue with being self-confi-dent—it was something she aspired to be. Only this guy was talking to Lyra in a way that was totally inappropriate.

"I've been cooking at the top bakery in New Jersey and am in line to be master baker very soon. I think we can agree that there are more men in that sphere, and I've worked harder to get there than most."

"Really? I find that women are on a par generally, and occasionally better, just as they are in every profession." Lyra's voice was cool. "Since you've been training so hard, we hope to see your very best, Mr. Thomas." With that she walked away, ignoring him when he called her name.

Louise gaped at Maddie, and she wasn't the only one echoing her "are you kidding me" look. The contestants were mainly women, but the other men shook their heads and looked down at their counters.

Meanwhile, the MC led Lyra to the small podium, and after a brief formal introduction and verification of the rules he handed the chef his microphone.

"I see that you're all eager to begin, so I'm not going to do a speech. Good luck and...let's get cooking!"

After the catch phrase Lyra always used on her shows, Maddie lifted the lid off her ingredients and pulled them out so that she could see and access everything better. Pulling out her recipe, she placed a large spoon on the top of it to keep it from moving and slipped on the apron provided.

First she turned on the oven and greased her cake pans, lining them with baking paper as well to ensure they came out easy and in one piece. Then she measured the dry ingredients into a bowl, including a cup of sugar, and gave them a stir. Next she melted butter, beat four eggs, and added both to a cup of milk and two cups of mashed banana.

Pouring the wet into the dry ingredients, she made sure they were totally mixed before three-quarters filling the pan. Smoothing the top, she placed it on a low shelf in the oven and set her timer.

Sparing the time for a quick glance around the room, she thought she was possibly the first to do so. It was too early to congratulate herself, but she did catch Dani's eye and shared a smile.

With time to kill, she cleaned up her station and put together the ingredients for a cream cheese icing with lemon and a butter cream filling.

A yell from across the room drew everyone's attention. Austin was cursing and had his hand under cold tap water. The producer and Dani were beside him in an instant and escorted him off the set. Maybe it was because they were nearing the end of the bake that no one seemed overly perturbed. More likely it was due to the time constraints and possibly that the injured was Austin. Maddie felt a little guilty at that, but like the rest she went back to the job at hand.

When her cakes were ready, Maddie pulled them out to rest and cool before de-panning them. Now it was a waiting game, and once more she glanced around to see how her timing compared with the other contestants.

Louise was on her knees peering through the oven window as if willing her cake to cook faster. Wiping her forehead on her shoulder, she noticed Maddie watching. "It's not cooked," she groaned.

"You've got five minutes," Maddie reassured her.

"It won't be enough."

Maddie feared Louise was right. Even if her cake cooked soon there would be no time to cool it before frosting. She didn't know what had gone wrong, but Louise would surely be out of the next round.

Sure enough, when the buzzer sounded, Louise had just pulled her cake out. It immediately sank in the middle. Tearfully she removed her apron and dropped it on the counter as Lyra arrived.

Maybe she didn't want to prolong the agony, whatever the reason, Lyra started with Louise. "What a shame you didn't finish. It sounded like a wonderful cake and I'm sure you've had better results. I do hope you'll try again in the future."

Louise's mouth trembled, though she managed a weak smile. "Thank you for the opportunity."

Lyra came to Maddie next. "I've had my eye on this cake since you frosted it, and I can't wait to try a slice." Maddie beamed and cut a slice, plating it with a flourish so that the soft frosting remained in place.

Lyra sliced her fork into it with a grin. "Nice." She lifted a decent piece and studied the texture. "Light and airy." Next she placed the cake into her mouth and closed her eyes. "Perfect. Well done, Madeline."

Filled with pleasure and happier than she'd been in months, Maddie watched her idol visit the other stations. Lyra was encouraging to each contestant while pointing out any faults, so there was no real idea how the competition was stacking up. It was nerve-wracking, but eventually the celebrity chef took the stage.

"This was incredibly hard and no matter the outcome, you should all be very proud of your cakes. In no particular order, the finalists are Tracey Leigh, Felicity Heron, Madeline Flynn, and Austin Thomas."

While Maddie kept her own counsel over the inclusion of Austin, murmurs of dissent rang around the room.

Lyra put a hand to quieten them. "I know this is irregular, but there is some question over the malfunction of the oven, Austin used. We feel in the interests of fairness, he should be given a pass into the final where he will use another station."

Maddie had a feel for people and she could see Lyra's smile did not reach her eyes. Obviously, as she was a stand in and it wasn't her show, Lyra wouldn't get the final say, but Maddie got the distinct impression that she wasn't a fan of this exception.

Back in the room, Austin glowered at anyone who so much as looked at him. If looks could kill, they'd be history, and Maddie gulped as she conjured up the spectacle of Cleo Black spreadeagled on the snow. Had the police discovered who killed her yet? She hoped so. Living below the apartment and walking by the spot each day filled her with dread. That might not go away, but it would certainly help once they apprehended the killer.

They had an hour break before having to bake again, and Maddie tried to call Dalton to see if he'd heard anything from the police and to make sure he wasn't at her apartment. As much as she didn't want to speak to him, she absolutely didn't want him to be there when she got home. It went to voicemail, and she wasn't sure if she was relieved or not. Anyway, she'd rather talk to Gran.

While telling her about getting through to the next round, Maddie deliberated whether to say something about the murder but decided against it. Gran would undoubtedly tell her to come home and as homesick as she'd been recently, her job was more important to her right now.

That determination helped make the decision not to say anything and combat her worry—just a little.

CHAPTER NINE

The final was close. She could sense, smell, and see it in the room. The four finalists were using the front stations and working feverishly. They had longer this time, and the cakes were bigger and more lavish. The theme was birthday cakes and Maddie had made hers with Maple Falls in mind. In particular, Gran's small farm.

After frosting, she had laid out a farm scene over the three tiers, complete with hay bales, fences decorated with balloons and flowers and the birthday girl in the middle dancing with a man. The fondant she was using for all the parts took a long time to fashion and color. The woman dancer was modeled on Maddie, but the man had a blank face so far. One thing she knew for sure—it wasn't Dalton.

On Maddie's left, Tracey Leigh struggled with her fondant over three tiers of a chocolate cake. Beyond her, Felicity Heron had one cake suspended over another as a hot air balloon and basket. It was proving to be a nightmare and Felicity was sniffing back tears.

Austin continued to glare at his competitors. He was immediately on Maddie's right, and the one time she caught his eye he sneered at her cake. She refused to look his way after that and hoped the others would follow her lead. No one needed the censure of a man like Austin, who likely didn't have a good thing to say about anyone.

As hard work and some luck would have it, Maddie's cake went according to plan, and the man gained some interesting features—an amalgamation of men she knew. Tracey wrangled her fondant with time enough to finish decorating. Felicity managed to complete hers too, though it had several cracks, and a few toothpicks could be seen holding the balloon together.

If karma was in action today all of it had fallen on Austin, whose cake was a castle that had, unfortunately for him, fallen on hard times. The color reminded Maddie of something from the bottom of a pig pen, and the flag flying from one of the half-finished turrets dripped the lettering into a circle around the base. It looked like a pool of blood.

Lyra started at Felicity's cake and sympathized over the lack of stability, praising her for the effort and risk involved. After tasting it, she moved on to Tracey's and exclaimed over the floral arrangement and the flavor. It was beautiful, and Maddie wouldn't be surprised if Tracey won.

Then it was Maddie's turn, and her stomach did a crazy somersault as Lyra studied each part of the cake. The time and silence seemed to drag until Lyra lifted an impassive face. And grinned.

"Maddie, this is stunning! I love how you've captured the farm lifestyle and incorporated it into the birthday theme. Is this you in the middle?"

"Thank you. Yes, it is." Maddie was blown away that Lyra could see the resemblance. "This depicts the party my grandmother organized for my 21st birthday."

"It's gorgeous and must have been a wonderful party." Lyra slid a knife easily into the cake and cut a generous slice.

She dropped it onto a plate in one deft movement, then swapped the knife for a fork and took a large amount to taste. Closing her eyes for a moment she smiled and moved on.

Maddie's stomach fluttered once more. *That had to be a good sign, right?*

"Now, what have we here, Austin? I can see you ran out of time to finish. Was it a little ambitious or did you have problems?"

"Not at all," he said dismissively. "The castle is a ruin, and you can see the decay…"

Lyra tipped her head and pointed at the crumbling turret. "Okay, but I can also see the cake in places where the frosting was too thin to stick, which is not what we expect for a finished item. Also, the use of colors isn't in keeping with a ruin, nor do I see any evidence of this being a birthday cake. What is behind the bake and who would this cake be for?"

"Well, I…anyone who likes history. Like me. I've been in the theatre you know?"

The chef nodded skeptically and sliced a piece of the best part of the castle. One that wasn't colored red. She tried a smaller mouthful than any of the others and swallowed hard. Wiping her mouth with a tissue she nodded. "It is rather dry, as expected, which explains the crumbling of your turrets." She didn't say more and moved away to the back of the room where she consulted a clipboard and made notes.

Austin stood fuming beside Maddie, his eyes carelessly spreading dislike around him. A finger of fear ran up her spine, clearly it was a repercussion from the murder and she squashed it quickly. He wasn't going to win, that much was obvious. If that was her, she would be looking for a way to pin a smile on her face. No one liked a sore loser, and sometimes things simply didn't work out.

They didn't have too long to wait, yet if felt like an hour

by the time the producer called the contestants to the front of the room where the MC and Lyra waited.

"You all did very well," Lyra told them in that sincere way she had. "Unfortunately, there can be only one winner of the $5,000 prize. However, since you've had to put up with me and not the lovely Ricardo, I have added consolation prize packs of tickets to one of my shows and my latest cookbook for the other finalists, with Ricardo's blessing."

This was such a wonderful and unexpected surprise that they all clapped and cheered enthusiastically—Austin not so much. Maddie would love to see one of Lyra's shows in person, and her cookbooks were amazing.

"All right, here we go! The winner is … Madeline Flynn. Congratulations! Your cake is an inspiration and not just for the taste and texture. Your decoration was inspired."

Momentarily stunned, Maddie stepped forward to receive the Perspex trophy with a gold plaque on the bottom bearing her name. She shook hands and Lyra encouraged her to hold it up for the cameras. While she had been hopeful, this was still surreal and right in front of her, Austin glared as if she had stolen it from him.

Maddie wouldn't let him spoil this moment. "Thank you so much," she said breathily, before being surrounded by Tracy, Felicity, and the other contestants who had rejoined them for the presentation.

"I knew you would win," said Louise, looking much perkier now it was all over. "Will we go for a drink to celebrate?"

"I'd love a quick coffee with you all, then I'd better get home."

Louise nodded knowingly. "You probably want to show off your trophy. I know I would."

Maddie smiled. There was no one other than Big Red she

cared to show it to until tomorrow. "You'll do better next time."

"I'm not sure I'm up to the pressure, but thanks for looking out for me." Louise smiled shyly. "It helped more than you know."

Tracey spread the word, and they traipsed out to the main street and around the corner to where Felicity knew of a cafe that was still open. She didn't notice him leaving, but it was a relief that Austin didn't come with them, and they had an enjoyable hour discussing the competition, the bonus prizes, and Lyra St. Claire in particular.

Felicity showed off her tickets proudly. "I'm sorry that Ricardo was ill but so glad we had Lyra fill his shoes and the chance to see her up close."

"Me too." Maddie glanced at her watch, and stood. "Thanks, everyone, for your kind words. If I go now, I'll make the next train home. I hope to see you all again soon."

They tried to delay her, but she was determined, and hurried to the station nursing her trophy, which was wrapped up inside her bag for protection. She was in line to go through the stile when a hand grasped her shoulder. Relief flooded through her when she saw the beaming smile. "Dani!"

"Fancy company on the way home?"

"Yes, please. I thought you'd be long gone."

"There's lots to do after the wrap. The space is rented and must be cleared out before we leave. I guess you didn't need anyone's help," she teased. "I can honestly say that we all agreed you were head and shoulders over the other contestants."

"That's so sweet of you to say." Maddie flushed happily. "There's always a certain amount of luck on the day. Good or bad."

"Hah! Don't tell me it was luck. Your cake was amazing, and I have proof that every member of staff thought so too."

"What kind of proof?"

"After they waxed on about the marvelous decoration, the crew proceeded to dig in and didn't leave a crumb of it. I can't say the same for any of the others, and no one touched Austin's."

Maddie was delighted that her cake was gone and had been enjoyed. And she wasn't surprised about Austin's cake. The thought of eating something so awful looking turned her stomach. "Ahh, out of curiosity, what did his cake taste like?"

"Sawdust."

"No!"

"It's true. Lyra had to drink two glasses of water before she could talk."

Maddie tried hard not to laugh. Of course, poor Lyra had to taste them all to judge the competition properly, which wasn't funny, but Dani was certainly entertaining. It was also a bonus to hear of things happening behind the scenes. She'd always wondered what was said about the bad baking, and now she could be glad hers hadn't qualified.

"Are you going to celebrate tonight?" Dani asked.

"I'm not a party kind a girl, and it'll be late by the time I get home. I'm sure my Gran will ring since I only had time for a quick call before we went to the cafe. I can't wait to tell her all about it."

"It had its moments of interest other than the cakes, didn't it? Lucky Austin didn't go with you, that would have spoiled things…"

"How did you know he wasn't at the cafe?"

"He was hounding Lyra and the producer for at least half an hour after you left. It wasn't pretty."

"Why would he do that after the winner was announced?"

"Beats me. Although, I think he was trying to get compensation for the burn. Not necessarily money from what I could hear."

Maddie frowned. "Was it really faulty equipment."

"Not on your life. He made a silly mistake by spilling cooking oil on the element and kicked up such a fuss the producer thought it easier to give him a pass into the final. It was right on every level that he didn't win, because the guy doesn't know much about kitchens and clearly can't cook worth a darn. In fact, I could bake a better cake than him, and that's saying something."

This time Maddie did laugh.

CHAPTER TEN

At the Manhattan station, Maddie toyed with ringing Dalton to say she was on her way, but in the end she went straight home because, frankly, she couldn't stomach talking to him. Ages ago he'd said he'd be okay to feed Big Red when she went to the competition, but she didn't trust him after their fight. She'd left plenty of food in case he didn't stop by and if she was late.

When she got to the apartment, the cat appeared out of the shadows before she got in the door. "Have you been waiting for me?"

He made some curious sounds that were decidedly unhappy, though he wound around her legs, clearly pleased to see her.

"Did Dalton feed you?"

Big Red hissed and the hackles on his back rose.

"I guess not," she muttered with relief and led the way upstairs.

But that relief was short lived when she heard music coming from inside. Darn it! If he hadn't fed Big Red, why was Dalton here? The answer was apparent as soon as she opened the door to find him and his friend, Mona Ridgley, wrapped around each other on the sofa. They were both so occupied they'd apparently not heard her come in. Maddie gaped, but Big Red leapt from the floor onto Dalton's back, claws extended.

Dalton wrenched the cat off him, which wasn't easy, and threw him across the floor.

"You leave him alone!" Maddie yelled and checked Big Red was okay.

Dalton scrambled to his feet. "Look at these scratches on my arm. I keep telling you that thing is vicious!"

Her fingers drummed fast and hard on her thigh. "Only to people who threaten me."

His eyes widened. "What do you mean? I'd never do that."

"I'm not talking physically. Listen, I don't want to argue tonight. It's time you both left. And Dalton, you better take everything of yours because you won't be coming back."

"That's a bit extreme. We can work this out."

His voice held an unappealing simpering tone that only served to annoy her further.

"Extreme? You're entertaining a woman in my apartment. There's nothing to work out."

"You weren't supposed to be back until later," he whined.

The distaste she experienced was overwhelming. "Are you kidding me? You think this is my fault?"

Eyeing her crossed arms, he gave her a hangdog look. "You're always busy or tired. What do you expect me to do?"

"Ever heard of being faithful, supportive, and unselfish?" she huffed. "They form the foundation for any decent relationship."

"You're being dramatic again."

He took a step closer, and she took one back while Mona watched the whole scene, something like glee glinting in her eyes.

"Dalton, get out of here right now before I call the police."

She undid her bag and began to empty it for something to do while they collected their things.

Dalton hesitated at the door. "You're going to be sorry you did this."

"I really don't think so, and I wish I'd done it sooner," she replied with no malice, just a good deal of regret over the waste of time in trying to make things work for someone who didn't deserve the effort.

"Take care, Maddie." Mona wiggled her fingers in Maddie's face swinging a bag over her shoulder and knocking the trophy to the floor on her way out. She continued with no apology, banging the door behind her.

A very rude word hovered on Maddie's lips as she picked up the trophy and turned it over, happy to see it was relatively unharmed. The plaque skewed to one side, and she righted it with a sniffle. No, she wouldn't cry over Dalton—he wasn't worth one tear.

After locking the door, she ran a bath and fed Big Red, who hadn't left her side and refused to, even when she climbed into the hot water. He curled up on the mat, close enough for her to run fingers through the soft fur. Sliding in up to her chin, she practiced a breathing technique Grandad had taught her. Thinking of him was bitter sweet, but this made her smile at least. He'd shared a good many things during her childhood. Some Gran had no knowledge of and the rest she turned a blind eye to. Things like self-defense and piecing clues together to solve puzzles.

All that training meant she could conceivably take care of herself in many situations. There had been no such tactics for relationships, which was a shame. Searching within herself, Maddie found a bruised ego and annoyance over the lost time spent with Dalton, but not much else. She couldn't get back the time, but she could certainly sooth her ego. She had a trophy, and she'd met her idol. It was a big day and a better day because of it.

People like Dalton weren't the majority. She had to believe that. He needed to be the center of attention, and women liked the way he looked. These were facts. Had there been other women before Mona? Closing her eyes, she slid under the water. What did it matter? Dalton was history.

When the water cooled, she dried herself and pulled on a pair of comfy pajamas and a thick dressing gown. Her sheepskin slippers, which had seen better days, completed the ensemble, and she padded into the kitchen in search of food. Being hungry was a good sign, but she was too exhausted to cook so instead quickly filled a bowl with cereal, added milk, and took it to the sofa. Feet tucked under her, she spooned up a mouthful and flicked on the television.

The news was on, and the first story began with a picture of a man causing chaos in Manhattan. Her stomach lurched as the slightly fuzzy photo came up. The snapshot of him zoomed in, and the bowl slipped from her lap to shatter on the floor. There was no mistaking it was Austin Thomas.

The news anchor spoke of his loss in the competition and how he had been unwilling to accept defeat. Apparently, the police were called to the set when he threatened Lyra and the producer. Later he'd taken assistant Dani Moon hostage and disappeared. Lyra and Dani's pictures popped up on the screen, and Maddie gasped.

"Dani's been abducted. That's not right!"

Big Red arched his back and hissed at the television, and while Maddie empathized she had already moved on to wondering how she could help. What could she do for Dani that the police weren't already? Probably nothing. Besides, she had no idea where Austin might take Dani, and the police would surely be there already—if they knew. Her mind whirred as it did when she had an itch to jump into action. She was miles away from where Dani was abducted.

Her stomach twisted again. That wasn't true. Dani rode back to Manhattan with her. She lived here, and from what she'd said about being tired, Maddie didn't think Dani would be doing any more traveling tonight. As scared as she was for her new friend, it occurred to her that if Austin had no idea where Dani lived—and why would he?—then he must have followed them to the station and boarded the same train.

She tapped her thighs with both hands as it occurred to her if Austin felt he had an axe to grind, the winner would be the one to be most resentful of. Wasn't that worse than being an organizer? And therefore, would Austin come for her next? He'd chosen to follow Dani, so unless she told him, he wouldn't know where Maddie lived. And if he wanted to hurt the organizers, would he now track down Lyra or the producer?

Big Red raced to the door just as a loud bang sounded.

CHAPTER ELEVEN

"It's Detective Bryant, Ms. Flynn. Can I come in?"

Heart still hammering, she stepped over the mess of cereal and checked through the peephole to make sure it was him despite recognizing his voice. Tucking her dressing gown closer she unlocked the door and let him in. He closed it behind him, face tight and a wary look in his eyes.

"Is this about Dani Moon? I just saw the news."

He blinked like an owl. "Do you know something about the abduction?"

She understood that he had a job to do yet didn't appreciate the gruff manner or the way he studied her like a specimen he couldn't quite name.

"I don't know a thing about what happened to Dani. She was involved in the competition I told you about, and we rode there and back together. We parted ways just outside the station, and I haven't seen her since."

"How long have you known her for?"

"We met for the first time this morning after I tripped and she caught me. We started talking and found out we were headed to the same place so we sat together on the train, but that's all." She was pretty sure the babbling made her sounded guilty of something but was powerless to keep her emotions in check. "Do you want to sit down?"

He nodded, eyeing the mess by the sofa, and sat in one of the kitchen chairs. "Did anyone else accompany you on the train?"

Grabbing a cloth from the kitchen she scooped up as much as she could. "I got a fright when I saw the news," she explained. He waited for her to continue and she took a moment to think about the question. "You mean Austin Thomas? He was definitely on it into Queens, but I didn't see him after the show. Dani mentioned that he was very unhappy with not winning, and that the cake he baked was, ah…not particularly well made. I guess he could have been on the same train home, but I thought he lived in New Jersey. At least, that's where he said he works."

"Do you recall if there was anyone else with him at any time?"

"Oh, you think he had an accomplice?" She gave the floor another wipe and dropped the cloth in a bucket under the sink before sitting opposite him, racking her brain for a familiar face. "There wasn't anyone I recognized on the train and he definitely seemed alone at the competition."

He made a note in the pad he'd extracted from a pocket. "It's over an hour each way. What else did you talk about?"

"Men." Maddie blushed at the way her thoughts kept rushing out. "At least we did on the way there. The thing is that it was Austin who bumped into me at the station this morning, although I didn't know who he was at that stage. I would have fallen if Dani hadn't caught me. He didn't apologize and was rude to everyone at the contest the entire day."

The detective's gaze didn't waiver. "So, you didn't like him?"

She shrugged awkwardly. "I don't know him at all, but what I saw didn't endear him to me or anyone else."

"Did you discuss how you felt about Mr. Thomas during the competition?"

"No, it was after the competition ended. We all went to a cafe nearby. And it wasn't an in depth conversation, but it was obvious that he'd upset most of them."

"So, how everyone felt about him is just conjecture?"

"My Grandad used to say, if it looks, smells, and barks like a dog, it probably is one," Maddie said tersely, growing tired of feeling guilty for something she wasn't responsible for, and having to defend herself seemed very unfair.

"I heard you won. That must have upset Mr. Thomas."

Maddie fumed some more, trying very hard to remember he was simply doing his job, and there was probably a procedure he had to follow. "It did, but I didn't win to upset Austin. Winning was one of the highlights, along with meeting Lyra St. Claire, and both were a surprise. The original judge was sick, so she shouldn't have been there."

His phone rang, and Detective Bryant removed it from his jacket pocket. He answered gruffly, the frown he'd perfected deepening. Having no wish to appear interested in his private conversation, Maddie moved into the kitchen to make coffee. He might not need it, but she definitely did. This was nerve racking and she hoped that he had people out looking for Dani.

She'd muted the TV, but something caught her eye, and the detective saw it at the same time. Video footage taken inside the station showed her walking with Dani along the platform in Manhattan. They were laughing. Several feet behind them a man kept pace. The image wasn't as clear as it could be, but good enough to make out Austin Thomas.

The detective abruptly ended his call. "That footage shouldn't be out there yet," he growled.

"So, this is how you connected the abduction to me. I was right; he followed Dani. What I don't understand is if he's after revenge, why did he take Dani and not me?"

His eyes narrowed. "You think he should have targeted you, since you won?"

"Don't you think it's odd that he didn't?" Maddie clapped her hands to her cheeks. "Unless he approached her at the contest thinking she could help him win and she refused and now he blames her."

"Why would he think that was a possibility?"

She grimaced as she remembered the awkward conversation. "Dani told me on the way to the contest that she was often approached by contestants looking for hints or tactics to secure a win and assured me that she would never use her position in that way."

He crossed the small room. "If you didn't know her beforehand, how did the subject come up?"

"When we discovered we were headed to the same place and in what capacity she explained how she felt about requests like that." Maddie gulped. "She wanted me to understand that our meeting didn't give me any privileges, which had truly never crossed my mind to ask for."

"Hmmm. So, you believe that Mr. Thomas tried to coerce Ms. Moon to help him win?"

Maddie shrugged. "It's one possibility. Although, I don't know when he would have had time. We were barely there for an hour before we began to cook on set and Dani was rushed off her feet."

He rubbed his fingers through his hair, and he looked tired. Oddly she felt sorry for him and wanted to help if possible.

"I assume the police also have footage of her being taken. Has he asked for a ransom or been in contact at all?"

He hesitated before answering. "It's not common knowledge, but a passerby witnessed the whole thing and took that video of the incident two blocks from the train station. That enabled us to get onto the case right away. As for a ransom— there's been no word. Has he contacted you?"

"No, he hasn't. Dani told me she didn't live far, and I wonder if Austin heard her mention that or already knew it. Maybe he thought if he got Dani alone he could make friends —and I ruined it by being with her when he might have had an opportunity to talk to her alone." Maddie halted mid-muse. "Do you think this has anything to do with Cleo Black's death?"

He leaned forward. "What would be the connection?"

When she couldn't think of a single one, the whiff of excitement evaporated, leaving Maddie feeling silly for mentioning it. "I guess it is far-fetched. Only, both cases seem so bizarre that for a moment they seemed to tie in."

"Having you as a common denominator would do that." He raised an eyebrow. "But not if the meeting with Ms. Moon was merely by chance."

She looked him straight in the eyes. "I can assure you that's exactly what it was. Do you have any leads on Ms. Black's murder?"

"You ask good questions, Ms. Flynn, but you need to leave it to the experts and not go off on a tangent to make sense of these crimes. Mr. Thomas is undoubtedly unstable, and Ms. Black's death is still under investigation, so I'll repeat that staying elsewhere until we deem it safe to return here would be for the best."

She nodded. After last night, she didn't want to be alone either. "I'll see if my friend will let me stay with her tonight, but I can't do it indefinitely. Big Red wouldn't like it."

His lips pressed together as if this was only way he wouldn't say what he was thinking about a cat dictating to his owner. The detective was clearly not owned by any pets, so he couldn't possibly understand. She tried not to hold that against him, since disbelief was common when she spoke of Big Red this way.

"I just wish there was a way to help Dani. She seems so nice, and I'd hate for her to get hurt when she was just doing her job and had no say over who would win."

"That's commendable, but the last thing we need is another victim." He stood and walked to the door where he turned with a frown. "Remember what I said. And thank you for your time."

When he was gone, Maddie shut and locked the door, leaning against it with a heavy sigh. The last few days had been hectic, and she was exhausted. The trouble was that she didn't think her mind would allow her to rest, and how could she go to work tomorrow and carry on as if nothing had happened? It had been hard enough after Cleo's death, but Dani might be alive somewhere, and the worry over how long the situation would continue, and what Austin's next move would be, bugged her.

Reluctantly she phoned Camille, who was naturally shocked and immediately insisted Maddie stay as long as she needed to. This should have been a happy day. The baking followed by the win had taken the edge off Cleo's murder for a time, but now the trophy was rendered meaningless. First by Dalton and his thoughtless actions, then by a stranger with a victim mentality.

Maddie packed an overnight bag and food for Big Red as Camille loved the big ginger lump and was happy to have him stay too. Ready to leave, she called Big Red and got no answer which was odd as he usually came running. She searched the apartment, which wasn't big so took no time at all, but with no luck. Where was he? She opened the door and called up and down the stairs, even tapping a can of food with a spoon, which was the biggest enticement she could think of.

Opening the window to the fire escape, Maddie peered out into the night. "Big Red? Where are you boy?"

She heard the normal sounds of cars and a couple of barking dogs, but no cat sounds. Sitting on the sill, Maddie swung her legs over and dropped onto the fire escape. Which way? She'd try up first. When she got to the window outside Cleo's apartment, she heard scratching and a plaintiff meow and could make out the large frame pressed against the window. Tugging on the sill, it didn't budge. Big Red was locked inside, and the how didn't matter right now.

Racing down to her apartment she found the little pocket tool set—a gift from her late Grandad. This time she went to the apartment via the inside stairs. Kneeling in front of the door, she had a moment's guilt, which she swallowed. The detective would not be happy with her, but she had to get Big Red out before he tampered with evidence. Who knew how long it would take for an officer to get here and unlock the door?

Pushing the yellow tape away from the lock, she slipped first one and then the other twig-like pieces of metal into the lock, teasing the release until it clicked. The door sprung open, and Maddie crawled inside.

Big Red sent her sprawling and she landed on her back to have a tongue rasp her cheek. He must have hated being stuck in here to act this way, and Maddie hugged him tight. "It's okay, I'm here, you big baby. She rolled over slightly and was about to get up when she spied something hanging from the underside of the kitchen table.

"What are you doing in here?"

Detective Bryant stood in the doorway with a gun in his hand and her hands shot in the air, which along with the fright he gave her made Maddie roll onto her back again, like a turtle.

Anxious he'd shoot her, she blurted, "Big Red was somehow locked in here and I, ah, managed to pick the lock." She might've simply said she'd opened the door, but there was no point in denying anything when the metal still hung from the lock.

"Any chance you like the thought of jail time?" he growled, holstering his weapon.

She shook her head, scrambling to her feet, noting how Big Red wrapped himself around the detective's legs. "I'm sorry. I know it's wrong in so many ways to be in here, but I panicked. I've organized to stay with my friend, like you said, only I couldn't find Big Red."

His eyes widened as he holstered his gun. "Are you suggesting you did this because of me?"

"Certainly not. Yours was a sound idea. I just couldn't leave him."

"Fine," he growled again. "Just get out of here, and I won't mention it, unless you do something like this again or it comes to light that you touched something you shouldn't have."

"I promise, I didn't. However, there is one thing you should know."

He rolled his eyes. "I don't want to hear any more of your thoughts or those of your cat."

"Do you want to hear about potential evidence?"

"Pardon?"

She crouched and pointed at the table. "Look. I noticed it when I fell on the floor."

Immediately he got down beside her. "What the heck is that?" Duckwalking the six or so steps the detective tugged a glove out of his pocket. Reaching underneath the table he pulled at the hanging paper, which turned out to be a small envelope. Slipping another glove onto his left hand, he opened it.

Maddie had followed the detective and was peering over his shoulder at that moment. Inside were pictures of Dalton with a couple of different men. "Why would Chloe have pictures of Dalton?"

"I think that's your best question yet, Ms. Flynn, and I aim to find out. Just as soon as you are on your way, which is incidentally why I'm back here. You don't instill any trust in me when it comes to your safety—or your ability to do what I ask." He slipped the photos back into the envelope and tucked them into his jacket pocket.

She grimaced but couldn't think of a suitable reply. It wasn't as though she hadn't heard that before.

CHAPTER TWELVE

I f she hadn't been so shocked at the photos, Maddie might have considered how kind the detective was to ensure she got to Camille's place safely, but she couldn't think straight, and no words came to her on the drive except to give him directions.

"Thank you," she managed to say as he dropped her at the apartment's entrance door along with her bag and a rather unimpressed cat.

"Go on, get inside before I leave, so I don't have to worry about you for the rest of the night. And don't walk around on your own at any time, okay?"

After Dalton's treatment, Maddie was inclined to give a snippy reply at being told what to do, but it was clear he had her best interests at heart, and it wasn't until Camille bundled them into her apartment that Maddie was able to enunciate her feelings. "I think Dalton is a crook." It was the first of many statements Maddie was intending to make, but Camille's retort stopped her cold.

"Well, sure he is."

"What do you mean?"

"He's as slippery as an eel and as charming as Jack Sparrow." Camille shrugged without apology. "I never doubted he was a shady character with ulterior motives for just about everything."

"Really? You never told me how much you disliked him."

Her friend snorted. "You never asked, but I'd like to think I made my feelings clear enough."

Like maple syrup on pancakes, the truth seeped through. They had known each other longer than she'd known Dalton, so of course she knew how Camille felt about him, and Dalton had certainly voiced his opinions about Camille being a man hater and a bad influence on Maddie.

Annoyingly, her lips quivered. How had she been so blind, ignoring the obvious and accepting Dalton was what he pretended to be—long after she knew he wasn't? That wasn't right either. She'd wanted the dream to stay alive, despite never needing a handsome prince on a white charger, because she didn't want to fail again by picking the wrong guy. All she wanted was to be seen for herself and not as a piece of clay to be molded into the ideal woman according to some outdated criteria.

Camille put an arm around her shoulder and pulled her down on the sofa. "Are you okay? Sorry, that's a dumb question after all you've been through."

"You don't know the half of it."

"Then you sit right there while I get wine and chocolate so you can tell me all about it."

Maddie didn't answer. Ordinarily she didn't touch alcohol during the week, but these were not ordinary times. Camille was a good listener, and maybe it would help order her chaotic mind if she went through everything in order.

Camille put a glass into her hand and opened the chocolate, waving it under her nose like smelling salts, which wasn't the worst idea.

She took a sip and picked up a piece of chocolate. "I don't know how, but Cleo Black's murder had something to do with Dalton."

Camille gasped and slopped wine down her sweater. "I know he's a snake, but murder seems out of his wheelhouse."

Maddie appreciated the sentiment, but Camille didn't have all the details. "You have to keep this to yourself—I found photos of Dalton in Cleo's apartment."

"When?"

"Just now. Detective Bryant caught me there just as I discovered them and brought me here because he figures I'm in danger." She didn't add that he didn't trust her to come by herself or that she'd broken into Cleo's apartment.

"Wow, Maddie, you sure don't let the dough rise before getting into the next problem. Who are you in danger from exactly?"

"That's just it. Dalton was doing something he shouldn't, and I'm his girlfriend. I mean, I was."

"That's better. For a second you had me worried. So, the person who killed Cleo wants to get Dalton now and potentially thinks they could get to him through you?"

"I guess. The trouble is I think the same about the crazy contestant who abducted Dani."

Camille tutted. "That makes no sense. He got who he wanted, right?"

"Maybe. But I won the competition, and Lyra St. Claire kicked him out. Aren't we guilty of upsetting him as much as Dani?"

"Sure, but he's hardly likely to kidnap three women, is he?"

"Good point." Maddie bit into the chocolate and closed her eyes. "Not unless he has help. Abduction usually means a ransom is imminent. He hasn't asked for anything yet, which is another worry."

"It only happened a few hours ago," Camille said reasonably. "Maybe he did it on the spur of the moment and hasn't thought this through."

"That is a possibility, yet he had to know that his face would be plastered on the TV. With traffic cams on almost every corner, he won't be able to hide for long." She groaned. "Unless he has a stockpile of food somewhere."

"Why would he if this wasn't pre-planned?"

"I don't know," Maddie admitted. "Because he's not right in the head?"

Camille snorted again. "And that makes a person stock up? If he was as arrogant as you said, there would be no way he'd think he would lose the competition or that Dani wouldn't help him if he had any doubts."

"You're right. That's the kind of man he seemed to be." Maddie took another sip. "I just hope they find her soon."

"And Dalton?"

"I would have thought he'd be easy to find, and it surprises me that they haven't yet. He's usually at work, my place, or the apartment he shares with his friends."

Camille screwed up her face. "Those idiots wouldn't be keen to help the police with their inquiries. Anyway, why do you look so worried about that?"

"Just because I don't like him anymore, I can't bring myself to wish him any harm."

"My dad would agree with you, but he didn't see the way that schmuck treated you. If he had he might have got the uncles involved."

Maddie shivered. The uncles could be scary, but she didn't like to think of them retaliating in any way more than verbally. "Do you mind if we don't talk about it anymore?"

"No problem." Camille smiled gently and handed Maddie the remote. "Here, you choose the movie."

The last thing Maddie wanted was for everyone to worry

about her, but she was grateful to have such a good friend. She clicked on the first movie that appeared and made room for Big Red to sit beside her. He snuggled in for all of five minutes before restlessly roaming the apartment. He'd been here before and knew which window led to the fire escape. He sat in front of it and gave her a pointed look.

Maddie dutifully did as he asked and opened the window then watched her cat pad down the stairs and around the corner of the building. It was a crisp night, but there was no new snow. It was also quiet out tonight. Very few people walked the streets and a line of cars stretched along the far side of the road indicating that the owners were tucked inside the apartments. Parking was at a premium because there simply weren't enough spaces, so people tended to get home as early as possible to park nearby so they didn't have to walk miles in the morning.

A light flickered in a car several down from the entrance of Camille's building. She pulled the curtain in front of her and peered around the edge of it. Was it a cigarette or a phone? Were they waiting for someone? Or watching—her?

CHAPTER THIRTEEN

"Camille, do you feel like a walk?"

"Have you lost your mind? What did you just tell me the detective said?"

"Not to go out alone." Maddie answered like a scolded child and not so sure she hadn't lost her mind.

"I believe he also said to stay home tonight."

"About that…"

Camille wagged a finger as her father did when he wanted to make a point. "No, Maddie. We are not going anywhere. There is now a murderer and a kidnapper out there, and you have no idea if you're their next target or not."

"I understand that it's scary," Maddie said soothingly, "but I promise I have no intention of being a target for anyone."

"Well, I don't know her, but I'd lay odds that Dani didn't have any desire to be one either. Look how that turned out when she strolled around Manhattan right after she upset that horrible man."

Maddie shuddered as she considered Dani's abduction. "She had no idea he was going to hold a grudge to that extent."

Camille crossed her arms and tapped a foot. "I rest my case."

"Fine. I won't go outside to check on the car right across the road from here that has a suspicious person in it looking up at this apartment as we speak."

"Do not try to convince me to go against my better judgement."

"I wouldn't dream of it."

"Hmmph." Camille fought the urge for a few more seconds before coming to the window and hiding behind the curtain next to Maddie.

"I see the shop on the corner is open still. They have decent ice cream, don't they?"

Camille glared at her. "They do."

"We'd be there and back in five minutes." Maddie assured her, but it looked like she'd played all her cards and lost.

"Five minutes and that's it. I'll get my coat."

Maddie hid a smile as Camille stomped to the bedroom. Shutting the window, Maddie shrugged back into her coat and wrapped a scarf around her neck while waiting by the door. Camille might be unimpressed with her guest right now, but they were unable to stay annoyed with each other for long, so Maddie knew she would get over it. Appreciating how she was always willing to help her, Maddie would make sure her friend stayed safe.

Besides, it was probably something innocent like someone waiting for a friend. All she wanted was to get a look at the occupant in that car so she could give the detective a lead via the license plate or a description if necessary.

They came out the front door arm in arm and crossed the road several cars down from the suspect. Maddie deliberately didn't look at the car until they neared it. Suddenly, the engine roared into life. The car swerved out into the middle of the road and shot around the next corner on the right.

They ran as fast as they could, arriving in time to see the taillights disappear around yet another corner. Maddie slapped a hand on her thigh. "I guess that means they were watching me and followed the detective and I here."

Camille swept her long dark hair out of her face. "Did you get a license plate?"

"Just the numbers," Maddie groaned.

"Cup."

Maddie frowned at her. "Pardon?"

Camille winked. "C-U-P. Those are the letters on the plate."

"How did you manage to see them once he pulled out?"

"What can I say? I have excellent eyesight." Camille shrugged. "It's a genetic thing."

Maddie hugged her and pulled out her phone. "Let's get back inside, and I'll call the detective on the way."

"What about ice cream?"

"Really? It's so cold tonight."

Camille sighed. "You're obviously not from around here. At this time of year, any temperature with a plus digit in it is warm."

Maddie grinned. Camille was certainly gutsy. "Alright already, get the ice cream—just hurry."

While Camille did that, Maddie repeatedly scanned the area. Who knew if the person watching them would return? She phoned the number the detective had given her, but his answer message kicked in, so she dutifully left the details. Hopefully he would get it soon. Should she dial 911 as well? The car was gone, and since there was no real threat yet, at least not that she knew of, the likelihood of the police coming to check it out was probably nonexistent. Besides, the detective would know what to do with the information, and she'd rather take his advice than a stranger's.

They were back in the apartment in no time, but immediately any relief about being inside slipped away. Big Red was also inside. He was clever—just not clever enough to unlock a door.

Camille made a weird keening sound. "How did he get in?"

"I was wondering the same thing." There being no point trying not to alarm her further, Maddie walked around the apartment and the bedroom before checking the bathroom.

Camille didn't move from where she'd stopped just inside the door. "Did you lock the window?"

Maddie nodded but checked anyway. "It's still locked." She went back to the door and checked both sides of it. "It wasn't forced, otherwise we would have noticed, but look at the scratch marks around the keyhole."

"Who the heck are you?" Camille exclaimed. "Some kind of spy?"

"Don't be silly. I just know some stuff."

Camille huffed at the brush off. "Stuff the rest of us don't know."

"Clearly some do." Maddie pointed to the marks as she yanked out her phone and tried the detective again. This time she had a better result.

"Are you inside the apartment?" he asked with no preamble. "I just listened to your message."

"Ahhh, I am now."

"What did you do?" Suspicion hung in the air, and Maddie gulped.

"Like I said, there was a guy in a car and I'm ninety-nine percent sure he was watching the apartment."

"Do you ever listen?"

She could almost see his gritted teeth. "I do try, but you have to admit it was suspicious."

"I told you to stay inside and call me if you saw anything."

"I wasn't sure that he was watching us. In fact, I didn't

know if it was a man or woman in the car, but they got out of there fast when we got close to it, which means we scared them off. And there's more. Someone's been inside Camille's apartment. I can't see anything out of place. Can you, Camille?"

Her friend jerked out of her trance-like state and glanced around the room. "I don't think so."

"She says no. What do you make of it?"

"If I knew that we'd be a lot further ahead with this investigation, and you wouldn't be left to your own devices."

"But you do think they're connected?" she insisted.

He groaned. "I don't know. There were no prints in Ms. Black's house, and they didn't have much time to look through your things. Unless you find anything missing, in which case give me another call, I suggest you get some sleep and I'll see you tomorrow. Do not go outside until then. I'm on another case, but I'll make sure whoever was watching you is replaced."

That was a surprise. She hadn't known that he had someone watching her and was relieved he was being proactive when there was so much conjecture around the case. His anger seeped through the phone, and she felt bad for the officer who'd messed up. "We won't. I promise."

"What now?" Camille asked, her voice shaking.

"We check all the locks and put the dresser in front of the door. Then we eat our ice cream and try to get some sleep. We've got work tomorrow."

"Sleep?" The word squeaked out like nails down a blackboard. "Who can sleep after knowing someone has been in here?"

"They didn't get anything, and there will be an officer watching the apartment from now on."

Camille crossed her arms. "That's not the point. I feel violated."

"Okay, I get that, but we were only gone five minutes. Hardly enough time to pick the lock, let alone rummage through your drawers."

"Stop! I don't want to think about that."

"Look, chances are we won't get any sleep, but we should at least get comfortable. Let's put on a movie and eat some ice cream," Maddie said pointedly.

Lucky it wasn't particularly warm in the apartment, because Camille still held the ice cream clutched to her chest. She looked at it in surprise and sighed heavily. "It won't help, but I guess we may as well."

CHAPTER FOURTEEN

$\int$ and paper rasped across her hand, and a weight pressed on her chest. Maddie jerked awake. "Must you?" she squeaked.

"What is it?" Camille's head popped into view, her eyes wide with fright in the still dark apartment.

"Don't worry. It's only Big Red telling me to get ready for work, else I'll be late." Once he'd clambered off her, Maddie stretched and yawned.

Camille yawned as well. "You're not seriously thinking of going into the bakery today?"

"I can't sit around hoping the police will solve this in a hurry."

"You're also in danger."

It was sweet that her friend cared so much, but Maddie was troubled that staying in the apartment meant Camille was in as much danger, and that wasn't right. "I'll be safer around people than waiting here like a sitting duck. That goes for you too."

"Oh." Camille screwed up her cute button nose. "I hadn't thought about that."

"Yes, if they can't get to me, then they might decide you could have some information."

Camille rolled off the mattress and stood, her face pale. "Information about what?"

Since Camille didn't want to sleep alone, they'd dragged the one from her bedroom into the sitting room last night and curled up to watch a baking show, eventually falling asleep.

"I don't know—what about how to find Lyra St. Claire? Or, what act of revenge would upset me the most?" Maddie shuddered at the idea of Dani being tortured somewhere out there and if Austin got hold of Camille, Maddie wouldn't be able to forgive herself.

And something else bugged her. Sometime during the night Maddie woke and got up to check on the car and what little she could see from the window of the neighborhood. The car hadn't returned and everything looked peaceful just the way it should. This got her thinking about Dalton and how nothing was resolved over his connection to Cleo Black. Every aspect of this was frustrating.

It was hard to get enthused for work which had never happened to Maddie since beginning at the bakery and she forced herself to snap out of it.

They were finally ready and had just stepped out the main door when a man in a dark coat, hat, and scarf came around the corner of the building. Camille grabbed her arm and Big Red hunched his back and hissed which turned out to be unwarranted. The man hurriedly pulled the scarf from around the lower part of his face. Not realizing she'd held her breath, Maddie exhaled when she saw it was Detective Bryant.

His eyes narrowed. "You gave me your word, Ms. Flynn."

"I recall promising not to go anywhere last night. However, it's morning and I must go to work."

"I need to talk to you, and it can't wait."

"Can we talk on the way? It's only six blocks."

"Very well." He nodded at Camille and walked between them. A man across the street wrapped his scarf tighter and kept pace with them. When the detective noticed Maddie's reaction, his mouth twitched. "It's okay. He's one of mine."

"Thank goodness you came. It was scary last night, and the thought of walking to work in the dark was giving me hives," Camille rambled.

Maddie wondered if she was fluttering her eyelashes at the detective, because she had that cooing sound going on. Detective Bryant took a step closer to Maddie, and she almost laughed. Yes, he'd heard it.

He coughed a little. "I was going to suggest you stay home today, but I figured you wouldn't listen, so hear me now—both of you. Mr. Acker was involved in something, this much we know for sure. Ms. Black was conducting an investigation—on him."

Maddie gasped. "You're not saying he had her killed?"

"I'm not confirming anything else except to say he is in custody. That potentially rules out any threat to you or Ms. Fournier from that quarter."

"Which leaves Austin."

"Exactly."

"If he has Dani, then isn't it unlikely he'll be cruising the streets looking for me?"

"He could have an accomplice."

"You don't sound convinced."

"As frustrating as it is for all of us, we simply don't have all the answers. Which means you must take precautions when I ask. It helps us do our job."

"I understand. Last night was simply because I knew you were elsewhere, and I thought if I could get the number it would help."

"It did," he conceded, "but it was very risky."

"I remembered half of it," Camille pointed out.

"Well done, both of you," he said dryly.

They walked the rest of the way in silence, and though Maddie wanted to ask questions, she knew he wouldn't give her any more details. It was frustrating, but his job was to protect them and it was clear he took that seriously. How could she blame him for not pandering to the amateur detective in her?

He stopped at the mouth of an alley. "I believe this is your bakery. Please don't leave it until your shift is done."

"We won't," Camille told him. "You can rely on me."

There was plenty of light from the shop to see Camille's eyelashes working overtime.

"I'd appreciate being able to rely on you both. My officer will be back to follow you home to Ms. Fournier's apartment. I'll be in touch when I have news."

"Why can't I go back to my place if Dalton is no threat?"

"Mr. Acker might not have killed Ms. Black, but someone did. I suspect he knows who that is."

"Then why wouldn't he tell you?"

"I'm pretty sure he hasn't put the two things together. We don't always know the people we feel closest to."

Maddie nodded soberly. She hadn't known Dalton half as well as she thought, and after catching glimpses she definitely didn't want to know the other side of him. That didn't stop her thinking about how he'd gotten involved with a murderer.

CHAPTER FIFTEEN

The family and staff waited less than ten feet inside the door. There was even a cake with "congratulations Maddie" written on it and underneath that was the word "winner." Her cheeks flushed as they clapped and cheered.

"You won!" Uncle Carlo clapped her on the shoulder. "We didn't doubt you would, not for a second."

Face flaming, she couldn't help a small grin as she rubbed her shoulder. "Thank you, everyone."

"Gosh, I had forgotten that," Camille exclaimed. "We should have celebrated at least a little."

"It's fine. I wasn't really in the mood, and it didn't feel appropriate last night. We'll have time to do that when this is sorted out."

"What is this?" Uncle Joey threw his hands in the air. "Why wouldn't you celebrate winning such a fancy competition?"

Maddie grimaced. "Unfortunately, the day ended badly."

"What do you mean?" Uncle Carlo didn't like drama.

The last thing she wanted to do was go over everything,

but the cat was out of the bag, and she owed it to the family to provide an explanation. They'd had faith in her ability to do well, encouraged her to enter, and given her the day off to compete, fully paid. Plus, they should know that Camille might be in danger. The thought made her stomach churn making it difficult to get the words out.

When she was done, the uncles gaped for several moments.

Uncle Roberto slapped a meaty hand on the counter, causing a puff of flour to coat his forearm. "This is not good. If a man is so angry about losing that he would kidnap a woman and track you down, then you and Camille are certainly not safe at her place or yours."

Maddie clasped her hands together to stop the strong urge to tap. "Before noticing the man in the car and having someone breaking into Camille's apartment, I honestly thought we were safe. I'm sorry to have involved her in this —I wish I hadn't entered."

Camille put an arm around her shoulder. "How could you have known that this horrible man would go off the rails and do something like kidnapping?"

Maddie loved that her friend held no animosity at involving her, but she couldn't forgive herself. "While that's true, I shouldn't have come to your apartment until I knew for sure that he wasn't looking for me."

"Where could you go? Your family is miles away," Uncle Carlo said gently.

"Family is the only place to go," Uncle Joey added. "Make no mistake, we are your family, and we take care of our own."

Maddie gave them all a watery smile. "You're all very kind, and I can't tell you how much I appreciate it. Now, I've taken too much of your time already, and I'd like to get to work if you're okay for me to be here."

"Of course, you must work. No one will harm you here—not while I have breath in my body!" Uncle Roberto growled and the others nodded vigorously.

"And you must tell us about your cake and show all the pictures. You have some, yes?"

"I do, Uncle Carlo. I'll show you when we have a break," she promised.

Satisfied, they went back to their stations, but every now and again she felt their eyes on her as well as poor Camille's. Her friend was stoic like her father and uncles, but she had to be scared. There was no denying that Maddie was.

For the whole day she pondered the crimes. Even cooking her favorite items and showing the photos of her creation as well as the trophy did little to take her mind off them. If anything, they were a reminder of the day, and she struggled to keep her emotions under control.

While Dalton's involvement in the murder was so far removed from Austin's obsession, it nagged at her that somehow they were connected in some obscure way. She had no proof, but Grandad also said she should trust her instincts, and he was never wrong about anything.

As Cleo watched Dalton and therefore Maddie's apartment, she would have seen people coming and going during the day and possibly at night. If Dalton was in bed with dodgy people, would he have brought them to her place? It seemed unlikely. Of course, he did bring Mona Ridgley. That thought made her skin crawl, though she appreciated that a lover and business deals were hardly the same thing. Surely, Cleo should have been staking Dalton's apartment instead. Or where he worked.

What if Cleo had done both? What if she'd seen him bring people to Maddie's apartment and intended to set a trap for Dalton? Only then would it make any sense for her to have rented the apartment above. Maddie hardly ever saw her come or go, which also made sense.

The piping bag she held suddenly squirted across a cake she was decorating when she squeezed it too tight. Darn it, she'd have to start again. There was a standard at Fournier's to adhere to, and she wouldn't let them down with a lack of concentration.

A standard. Dalton had to do things by the book. Obviously he hadn't been, so he was undoubtedly facing jail time. The question was, did he do something fraudulent, which was bad enough, or did he really commit murder? It was hard to imagine that he'd had time to run upstairs and push Cleo out the window. The detective didn't think he had been involved, although he never said it was an absolute.

The idea that she'd spent nearly two years with a crook and a would-be murderer made her stomach roil yet again, and she raced to the bathroom. Washing her face with cold water, Maddie looked in the mirror at the pale face filled with disbelief that she'd been so blind to the real Dalton.

The darkness around her eyes told the story of not just one bad night's sleep. If she was going to figure this out, she needed to rectify that. Which was easier said than done with all these thoughts racing around in her head.

She also needed to find out where Dani was. The guilt was eating at her. The trouble was she couldn't do anything about it if she wasn't able to go anywhere but the bakery or Camille's apartment.

At her lunch break, she was presented with a plate of garlic bread and a bowl of soup by Uncle Roberto. "My wife made enough for everyone. You don't come back to work until it's all gone."

It wasn't a suggestion. She took a tentative mouthful, and her tastebuds went into overdrive just as her phone rang.

"Maddie?" A timid voice asked.

She clutched the phone and her heart raced. "Dani? Is that really you?"

"Yes," she spoke just above a whisper. "Are you okay?"

"I'm fine. Where are you? Are you alone?"

There was an audible gulp. "I don't know where I am. Austin left not too long ago and locked me in again. I waited a bit before I phoned in case he came back."

It was odd that after going to the trouble to kidnap Dani he would then leave a phone in reach. Still, he might be back at any moment, and she wouldn't waste the opportunity to help and didn't intend to scare Dani by making that point. "That's okay. Let's figure this out together. Tell me anything you can hear or what you remember from how you got there."

"He was waiting for me at the entrance to my apartment. It doesn't have a doorman, and before I could get in the foyer, he dragged me into his van, which was parked right outside. He had a cloth in my mouth, and I couldn't scream. He put one over my nose as well, which must have had something on it, because I was out cold pretty fast and didn't see how we got here." A sob came through the phone.

"I guess you didn't notice if anyone saw this happen?"

"It happened so fast, and the awning over the door is wide and covers most of the pavement, so I don't think anyone was around, otherwise they would have helped, right?"

"Mmmm," Maddie murmured, thinking that not everyone had a conscience. "Do you remember anything else?"

"It was dark and quiet by the time I came around, and I was on the floor in here."

"What does the room look like?"

"It's an old place. Dirty and rundown. There isn't any furniture except a broken chair. I'm so scared, Maddie."

"As soon as I get off the phone, I'll call the detective," she promised.

"No! Don't hang up. I may never get another chance to speak to anyone. I swear my phone was dead, but when I tried it just now it worked. There's only a couple of percent left so I don't know how much longer I've got."

A part of Maddie wished Dani had called 911 instead, but she heard the panic and didn't want to stress her any further by pointing this out. "All right, let's concentrate on what you can see. Is there a window?"

"There are four, and they're all boarded up. I can hear cars nearby but no voices. I banged on the door for ages the first time he left—no one came." She sobbed again. "The posters on the wall are frightening."

"Posters?" They could be for a warehouse or factory and might have a name on them or some kind of clue. "What do they look like?"

"They're all for horror movies. Really old ones. All of them are peeling off the brickwork."

Maddie had an idea, and she was already on the way through the kitchen. "Are all the walls brick?"

"Yes." Dani sniffed. "And there's a funny smell."

"Like smoke?"

"Yes, that's what it is! Some of the walls are blacked too, as if there's been a fire."

"I think I know where you are. Last time Austin left, how long was he gone?"

"Oh, thank goodness. This is the third time he's been gone. When I woke up he let me use a bathroom then locked me back in here. He hasn't let me out since." Dani's voice filled with hope. "This time he's been gone for ages. Maybe he's given up on whatever his plan was."

Maddie chose not to disagree. It wouldn't help. "I'll be there as soon as I can." Her stomach tightened. She had better not be wrong about the location.

"Camille, I need help!" Maddie yelled across the kitchen stopping most of the staff in their tracks.

With no hesitation, Camille came running, a whisk dripping across the spotless floor and it occurred to Maddie that the uncles might not be happy with her hastily conceived plan.

CHAPTER SIXTEEN

L uckily a cab stood at the curb. Maddie shouted the address and bundled herself inside. "Hurry! It's a matter of life and death."

"Maddie? Are you still there? The battery's showing one percent!"

Panic was setting in for Dani, and Maddie wasn't far behind her. "I'm nearly there. Let me call the police."

"No! What if you're wrong? Please. Keep talking."

About what? Maddie urged the driver on, then told Dani how she'd run out of the bakery and wondered if she still had a job. Her bosses were sticklers for performance and punctuality, but they were fair so perhaps they would understand. She was rambling, but it was the best she could do. Meanwhile, Dani breathed heavily, and by the sound of footsteps, she was pacing a decent-sized room with good acoustics.

The cab swung around a corner, and Maddie slid along the seat. "I can see the building," she gasped as the driver squealed to a halt outside an old theatre.

Up until the fire a year ago it had been the place where

classic horror movies were shown on a regular basis and before that, in it's heyday, it hosted all the great shows.

She threw money at the driver and leaped out of the cab. "Call the police!" she yelled.

The large double doors were barred, so she ran to the left and around the corner where she found a couple of boards broken over a window. Hauling herself up and through, she landed hands first on the soot-laden floor. Keeping as still as possible, blood pounding in her ears, she listened for any sounds of Austin. A different kind of pounding ahead of her grew insistent, and she sprang into action in the murky light coming through several more boarded up windows.

"Hello? Hello? Is anyone there?"

The relief at knowing Dani was safe felt overwhelming. "It's me," Maddie called, spying the key that dangled enticingly from the lock, and nervously she glanced around the room. As far as she could make out, the place was empty and there was little to hide behind. With a deep breath she unlocked the door and swung it open. Dani backed away a couple of feet, then pounced on Maddie, wrapping her arms around her so tight she struggled to breath.

"I don't know how you did it, but thank you for finding me." Dani sobbed into Maddie's shoulder.

Gently prying her loose, Maddie smiled. "I'm so glad you're okay. Let's get out of here."

"Oh, you're both leaving all right." A familiar figure loomed in the doorway. "With me."

"Austin!" Maddie squeaked as Dani grabbed her arm with a moan, nails digging into her skin.

Austin simply grinned, clearly enjoying their fear at the gun he pointed at them. "Surprise. I knew you'd come."

Furious at her stupidity, Maddie glared at him. "You left the phone on purpose."

Dani's grip tightened. "I'm so sorry, Maddie. I truly didn't know. Just before he left he said he was coming after you. When I saw that he left the phone and it was working again, I had to warn you."

"Don't blame yourself for this. You were scared, but you also phoned the police, right?" Maddie narrowed her eyes willing Dani to say yes, no matter that she knew it was a lie.

Dani blinked. "Of course. They should be here at any moment."

His laughter was ugly. "Nice try. I charged her phone just enough, and unfortunately for you she only made the one call. He nodded to a vent above them. "I never left the building. If she had called the police, I would have simply moved on. With or without her."

The threat in his voice made his point abundantly clear. He wasn't bothered if he had to kill Dani, which meant she was merely bait. It also meant he wanted Maddie more.

"Maybe she didn't, but other people like the taxi driver did."

Eyes narrowed calculatingly, Austin held his hand out to Maddie. "Speaking of which, give me your phone—now!"

A fleeting thought about how she might wrangle the gun from him stalled before she reluctantly handed it over. She simply couldn't risk him firing and hurting Dani.

He snatched it and thrust it into his jeans pocket. "Enough chit-chat. We're going for a little walk, and you better not try anything funny. Either of you." He pointed behind him to the door, and when they walked through it he directed them to the corner. Painted in a brick pattern, there was a door she hadn't noticed. He gave her a key to unlock it, then pushed them through and locked it behind him.

"Get down the stairs." He grabbed Dani's arm so that she was the one immediately in front of him. At the bottom there was a dark opening. "Don't stop," he warned.

Maddie shuddered when her fingers touched the edge of a dark tunnel. "What is this place?"

"It connected the dressing rooms with the theatre and leads to a very private exit for the players who didn't want attention. It was a good find when I did some amateur theatrics. No one likes the villain," he gloated. "Though, I didn't think I'd ever use it in quite this way."

He pushed Dani into her hard, and Maddie forced herself to walk slowly forward, thinking of other ways to stall him in case the cabbie had called the police like she'd told him to do. "Why do you hate us so much?"

"Are you stupid?" He sneered. "I was supposed to win that competition! Instead, you all conspired to rob me of my chance to shine."

Maddie skidded to a halt. "How do you figure that? I won fairly, and all Dani did was not allow you to cheat."

"Fairly? Dani could have helped put in a good word with Lyra, if you hadn't got to her first. Besides, if I hadn't burned myself I would have won. I couldn't work properly," he whined.

"Your hand looks okay to me," Maddie pointed out rashly.

"I heal quickly," he growled. "Now if you don't want Dani hurt, shut up and get going!"

Austin was delusional—this much was obvious. He thought he could win a competition without actually competing and was determined to blame everyone else for his failure. Her heart sank as she remembered the way he had knocked her over at the station. If he'd seen them sit together he must assume there was some collusion involved, and she could see there would be no way to talk her way out of what he'd decided was the truth.

She still didn't hurry as the tunnel grew steadily lighter, which meant they were almost out of time, and in a few more seconds they entered a smaller room. Yet another door needed unlocking and then they were out in the street in a narrow alley. A van straddled the curb, and Austin slid open the side door. Dani shivered, her glance lingering on Maddie, who wracked her brains to think of something, anything, that might give them a fighting chance.

"What do you want from us, an apology?" Maddie spoke loudly in case any rescuers were waiting for them.

"Words can't fix this." He snorted. "What I want is for you to help me get Lyra St. Claire to admit her mistake. Put these on your wrists." Austin handed Dani four plastic ties. "Do Maddie's first, then your own."

"Even if I wanted to, I don't have a contact for her," Maddie protested.

"I believe Dani does."

"You know I have her number, but you tried it already, and when her assistant Maggie Parker answered, you hung up," Dani blustered.

Austin shrugged. "If she heard my voice, it was unlikely she'd hand the phone or a message to Lyra. No, this time your new friend Madeline Flynn can phone Lyra. I doubt your number will be recognized." He pulled out her phone. "Password?"

She had no choice but to tell him, and he keyed it in, then the number from Dani's phone. It rang several times before a woman answered.

"Maggie Parker. How can I help you?"

Austin held the phone to Maddie's face and nodded for her to speak as he held the gun against Dani.

Maddie licked her lips. "Hi, Maggie. I don't know if you remember me. It's Madeline Flynn."

"Of course, I remember you. Congratulations again for your win. What can I do for you?" She sounded friendly.

"I wonder if I might have a quick word with Ms. St. Claire?"

"She's busy right now, but I can take a message."

Austin pressed the gun into Maddie's side, making her gasp. "It's an urgent matter."

"Oh." There was a pregnant pause. "Let me put you on hold a moment, and I'll see what I can do."

Austin grinned. "Very good. When she answers, ask Lyra to meet you at your apartment. Tell her you have information regarding Dani and don't know who to trust."

Maddie's eyes widened. "Lyra might not still be in town, and she certainly won't come to my apartment."

"Oh, she's still around. She'll want to save her career from more bad publicity, so she'll do whatever she must. Trust me."

That was the last thing Maddie would do. "Then what?"

He smirked. "Let me worry about the finer details."

CHAPTER SEVENTEEN

"Hello, Maddie. It's good to hear from you. I've been so worried about you and the other contestants since I heard about Dani. Is that what you're phoning about?"

The gentle voice disconcerted her. "I'm sorry to say it is. I wish I didn't have to involve you, Ms. St. Claire, but I need your help to save Dani, and I can't go to the police, no matter what Detective Bryant said. You've probably heard from him —he's the one leading the investigation."

"Yes, he's been in touch a couple of times, but I had nothing to tell him. I do feel so responsible and will help in whatever way you need to find Dani."

Maddie almost gagged at how little persuasion she needed to use to get the famous chef to step into danger. It wasn't right, but what else could she do? "Thank you...for taking the call and for helping me win the competition. I can't say much now, but could you come to my apartment in an hour?"

Apart from Austin's rapid breathing in her ear, there was a considerable silence, and Maddie wondered if she'd scared her off with the rushed explanation and desperate tone.

"Sorry," Lyra finally spoke. "Maggie is already organizing a car. I'll come directly."

Anxious and yet relieved, Maddie told her the address. "Please come alone and don't call Detective Bryant."

"All right, if you think it best." There was a pause. "Are you okay?"

She didn't need to look at Austin to know he'd watched her during the exchange and standing so close he'd heard every word. Maddie swallowed hard. "I'm fine." *So far*

"Good. Stay safe and I'll see you in an hour."

The call disconnected and Austin pocketed the phone. "See. I told you she'd come. Let's hope she does come alone. For yours and Dani's sake. Now both of you get into the van."

This was easier said when they couldn't use their hands, and again he gave them both a shove and they ended face first on the floor of the disgusting vehicle. Maddie's stomach rebelled. A real chef wouldn't be happy being surrounded by discarded takeout containers and half-eaten food.

She rolled to her side and took stock of their prison. The windows were blacked out, so she wouldn't be able to get anyone's attention. Maddie made it into a sitting position before he took off. For someone who was laying low, he wasn't exactly a careful driver. The plastic tie bit into her hands as she rolled from side to side, and a couple of times Dani fell against her with a whimper. Still gagged, Dani frowned and tilted her head.

"I know you want answers to how we're going to get out of this," Maddie whispered in her ear. "Right now, I don't know, but it will be okay." It wasn't a lie, but she sounded a good deal surer than she felt. All she had was hope that Lyra would do the right thing with the information she had. And that at some stage Maddie could get the upper hand over Austin. If he let his guard down she had to be ready to escape.

She shuffled closer to the grill separating the back of the van from the front and peered through the metal. Austin was already pulling up to the back of her apartment blocks, and in a few seconds he stopped the engine. Turning in his seat, he eyed them both.

"You keep quiet in here," he snarled at Dani. "While Maddie and I introduce ourselves once more to Lyra St. Claire. Any fuss from either of you and you know what the result will be."

When Maddie nodded he got out and opened the door beside her. Unceremoniously he yanked her out. She almost fell onto the sidewalk but managed to keep upright by awkwardly grasping the side of the van with both hands.

"I'll remove the tie, but remember I have this." He thrust the gun into her ribs.

She nodded again, licking her lips, and swallowing in case an opportunity to call for help arose. Once they got away from Dani, there would be one less pressure to keep silent.

He draped an arm around her shoulder, dragging her firmly into his side and she felt the gun more keenly.

How could she slow him down to give her a chance to be seen? "The basement door is always locked."

"I know." he smirked. "Along with the last fire escape section."

He'd obviously done his homework, and Maddie nodded trying not to look so pleased about his dilemma. That left only one way in.

The alleyway between the two buildings was dark and eerie, although she could hear children's laughter seeping through the windows above. A snowflake fell on her eyelashes, then another as they walked toward the main street. Austin hesitated at the corner to peer around the brickwork. One heartbeat, maybe two, then he pulled her with him.

Maddie slowed her steps, and he growled in her ear. "Don't think about it."

The stoop was only a few more feet. Was this her last chance before they got inside? A woman and a small girl holding hands crossed the road in front of them and both smiled at her as they went by. She couldn't involve them and held her breath, only exhaling once they'd moved on. The moment and perhaps her last chance to get away was lost.

He pushed her up the stairs, into the entrance way and on toward the staircase. Side by side they climbed to the second floor.

"Key," he demanded. "Slowly."

After pulling the keyring out of her pocket, she shook so much Maddie had to use two hands to get it in the lock. Once opened, he shoved her ahead of him and slammed the door behind them. "Get on the sofa and don't move."

"Finally." Mona Ridgley sauntered casually out of the bedroom.

Austin's reflexes were much quicker than she'd guessed. "Drop the gun!" He swung and pointed in one gesture.

Mona's eyes bugged as she noticed he had one too, and it was much bigger. She dropped hers like a hot potato. "Who the heck are you?"

"I might ask you the same."

Mona hesitated and then a cunning light came into her eyes as she smirked at Maddie. "I'm a friend."

"Yeah, and I'm Santa Claus," Maddie muttered, not sure what to make of the new development.

Austin briefly considered the exchange. "What do you want with her?"

"It looks like the same thing as you. Our 'friend' here takes too much notice of things that don't concern her, which has made her rather unpopular. She's also struggling with her boyfriend dumping her, which is probably why she's so depressed." Mona winked. "Did you know she takes sleeping pills?"

Austin grinned. "Well, well, well. Thanks for the insight. I'll remember that when the time comes. Right now she has a job to do, and you need to keep out of my way."

"In case you haven't guessed, I'm not here to do her any favors." Mona's eyes sparkled. "What kind of job?"

"She has a visitor due soon, and they must meet. It's a case of life and death."

Maddie shuddered at his maniacal laughter and, to make things worse, Mona joined in.

"I guess we both have her best interests at heart. Need any help?"

"Nah, I've got this. Unless you want to make coffee for two and hand over the pills. Maddie and her guest will be thirsty, so it will be the perfect opportunity for them to rest up afterward."

"Sure." Mona winked. "I make a mean coffee."

"Where's Dalton?" Maddie half expected him to come through the door as happy as his girlfriend over her predicament.

"If you must know, he's at my place where he belongs."

"As if I didn't see that coming. Doesn't he ever go home?"

"He's between places right now, if you must know," Mona said conversationally as she made the coffee. "Anyway, we're moving in together permanently now that his last job is done and he doesn't need you as cover."

This wasn't nearly enough detail and with an effort, Maddie leaned back casually. "How nice for both of you. I'm sure it's all legitimate, or he's gotten better at swindling people. I guess using my place kept any upset clients from tracking him down."

Mona shrugged. "It's not the kind of place a man like Dalton would be expected to hang out, and it's not Dalton's problem if people are dumb enough not to check what they're buying."

The fact that he had used her place was upsetting enough, but if he had people after him, then she was in danger and for Dalton to put her in that position was gut wrenching. Clearly he had never loved her and their whole relationship was a lie. How had she been so stupid to fall for a con artist—a man who cared nothing for her safety.

She gulped as it hit her—danger was coming thick and fast from all directions. Her attention switched from Mona to Austin who had been checking every inch of the apartment. He turned and she caught the look of speculation directed at Mona until he spied the trophy on the counter.

Gently he caressed it with his gun. "What happened to this?"

Maddie narrowed her eyes. "Ask Mona."

The antagonistic woman snickered. "It had an accident."

He didn't seem impressed and a rap at the door interrupted her gloating.

"Maddie? It's Lyra."

Maddie jumped to her feet, but Austin waved her back, nodding to Mona who shrugged and did as he bade. Pulling the door open, she hid behind it while Austin stood a few feet back, gun pointed straight ahead.

"Don't come in. It's a trap!" Maddie screamed

Only, it wasn't Lyra who came through the doorway. Detective Bryant rushed in; his gun pointed at Austin. "Put the gun down and your hands in the air!"

Austin's mouth gaped. "Who…?"

"Gun down, now!"

"I don't think so, Detective. You're outnumbered, so drop your weapon," Mona shrieked and came from behind the door in a rush.

Surprised, the detective swung quickly toward her. The

horrifying sound of gun fire reverberated in the small room and the detective dropped to the floor and lay still. Before Mona could get off another round, Maddie leaped across the coffee table and threw herself at the horrible woman. They fell together in a heap against the wall.

Breath knocked from her, Maddie held onto Mona with everything she had while the woman tried to claw her face with pink talons. Another shriek came from across the room, and before Mona was hauled off her, Maddie saw Austin tearing at a ball of ginger fluff attached to his head.

Big Red meowed loud and terrible, and Mona spat foul words beside her, where another officer held the woman's arms pinned to her side. Yet another officer plucked Austin's gun from the floor while Maddie crawled over to the detective and desperately felt for a pulse.

CHAPTER EIGHTEEN

There it was—fast but steady. Maddie rolled the detective onto his back and undid his jacket to reveal the thickness of a bullet-proof vest, which had stopped the bullet exactly over his heart.

With a grunt, his eyes flickered open, and he sucked in a deep breath. "Arrgh!" He clawed at the vest, the area around his mouth turned white, but at least he was alive.

She helped him remove it. "I'm glad the vest saved your life, but you gave me one heck of a fright."

"I hardly think this makes us even," he managed through gritted teeth as he rubbed his chest.

Maddie flushed a little at the justified censure. No, she hadn't stayed out of danger as he'd insisted, but surely this was a good result. Everyone was where they were supposed to be and safe, weren't they? Glancing around, she had a moment of panic. "Where's Lyra?"

He pushed himself up with a groan. "As if I'd bring her here with a killer on the loose."

"Good point. Still, she must have phoned you, right?"

"She didn't have to. I was with her when you phoned. I

figured when you went missing it was just a matter of time before Austin contacted Ms. St. Claire, since he clearly blamed all three of you for his failed attempt at stardom. Your celebrity chef sends her best, and to be honest she would have come if I'd let her. I figured one rogue baker at a time is quite enough for the police to deal with."

The words were cool, yet there was a twinkle in his eye that made her think he wasn't as mad as he wanted to be. Maddie cupped a hand to her ear. "Sorry, I'm finding it hard to hear you."

He shook his head at this pathetic attempt at deflection and raised his voice. "Perhaps you should call your cat. He seems to have gone feral."

He was right, but she couldn't stop a grin. Kidnapper and killer were now in cuffs, with Big Red still hissing and carrying on in front of those two, much to the amusement of the officers.

"That's enough, boy," she said firmly. "You did a great job."

Big Red hissed one more time and slowly backed away—but not too far.

The detective chuckled. "That is some guard cat."

"He certainly is," she acknowledged, happy that every-thing was sorted out, until she remembered something that required their urgent attention and hurried to the door. "We still need to set Dani free! She's locked in Austin's van."

He waved a hand, the other still pressed to his chest. "We found her. She's safe and waiting outside with some friends of yours."

"I can't tell you what a relief that is. Is she okay?"

"Thanks to you, she's fine, just a little shaken."

Maddie came back and slumped onto the sofa. Big Red finally left off guarding the culprits and jumped on her lap to nuzzle her cheek. Surely it was over now, except for one last culprit. "Dalton—did you find him too?"

"No need to worry about him either. We're taking good care of Mr. Acker."

"So you found out about his business dealings?"

He sucked in a breath and stood. "What do you know about them?"

"Nothing, except that Mona alluded to them going bad and that he was involved in something big."

"You might say that. Did she happen to say what part she played in them?"

"I got the impression that she wasn't as involved in Dalton's dealings as she was in her obsession with him. Whether that was about money or his charming personality, I couldn't guess."

"Hmm. I'm sure you could," he muttered. "We'll need another statement from you concerning everything you've been involved in or have even the slightest knowledge about."

Maddie nodded. This could take some time, and she was exhausted. "Could someone give me a ride? I don't have a car."

"I don't think that will be a problem. You could come with me, only there's a bunch of people outside with Dani and they're ready to do battle for you. We had to threaten them to keep them back and I'm sure they'd only be too happy to drive you."

"Really?" Maddie would be surprised if they'd had time to get Gran or her friends out here from Maple Falls. "Who is it?"

He nodded at the window. "See for yourself."

Sure enough, on the opposite side of the street, Camille and the uncles stared up at the apartment. They saw her immediately and waved frantically. Camille jumped up and down, shouting something Maddie couldn't hear, but she waved back just as enthusiastically. Then the family stilled.

Pressing her face to the cold glass, she saw Mona and Austin being led to two separate police cars below.

A crowd had gathered along the sidewalk near the family, and some must have recognized the kidnapper from the news, as there were a few gestures and finger pointing. And when they spied Maddie, that became more intense. They barely knew her, but a muttering gained momentum and volume, seeping through the window, and though she couldn't pick out any words she felt the sentiment through every fiber of her being. They did not need or want people like this in their neighborhood.

"Are you ready?" The detective waited by the door holding her coat.

His gentleness, when added to the adrenaline slipping from her body, brought up a wave of self-pity. Or maybe it was relief. She sniffed, hoping it was the latter. There was no way she would mourn Dalton's capture. If he was a thief, he deserved jail time, and even if he was simply a terrible boyfriend who'd been targeted by a stalker with no conscience he wasn't worthy of tears.

They got down to the street where the press, and those spectators who felt they had a right to answers, pushed at the line of officers barring their way.

"Maddie! We hear you know both people in custody. Are they also the killers of Chloe Black?"

"Don't answer them." Detective Bryant moved in front of her to shield her, which didn't stop a microphone on a pole being thrust into her face. "I think it best you come with me."

"Were you involved in the killing or the kidnapping?" A man boomed at her.

She swung to face him. "No, I was not!"

Before she could do more, Bryant put an arm around her shoulders and dragged her to a waiting car. He slipped in beside her as she moved across the back seat, stunned at the suggestion.

"Do people really think that?"

"I won't lie, there are always people out there ready to believe anything, and the press can easily taint the truth if they choose. There is absolutely no point in worrying about that. The facts will be released when we have all the information and the people who know you, or care about those facts, will know you're innocent."

Though she didn't like that people would judge her wrongly, she knew he was right about the inability to change their minds. She'd been a determined people pleaser until she fought for the career she wanted. And when she finally saw through Dalton, she realized that she was the one who'd changed. She'd enabled him to walk all over her, because she didn't think she deserved better. While she had no inclination to look for a new boyfriend, and couldn't imagine doing so anytime soon, a man would never treat her that way again.

Maddie knew she was wiser and stronger for this experience and while that didn't make it worth the anguish and fear, taking something good from it certainly helped.

They slowly passed by the Fourniers, who waved, and Maddie pointed back at the apartment block. "Big Red," she mouthed. Camille gave her a thumbs up and Maddie sat back with a heavy sigh. The ginger terror deserved many treats after the way he had helped today.

CHAPTER NINETEEN

I t was going to be a late start this morning, despite getting to work on time. The uncles and Camille were fussing over her, and the rest of the staff wanted the full story.

After the interview and her statement was taken, Maddie stayed the night with Camille again at everyone's insistence. Detective Bryant, Camille, and the uncles wouldn't take no for an answer, and to be fair she barely raised an eyebrow. Not only did she not want to be alone, but her apartment was also involved in the investigation and off limits for another day or two, making it an easy decision.

She'd had a few moments with Dani, who made her swear to keep in touch, and looked forward to that. Plus, Detective Bryant said he would check on her, which was sweet of him. Maddie smiled. It turned out he was even nicer when he wasn't in detective mode or annoyed with her.

It had come as no surprise that Mona was a serial stalker, and Dalton had fulfilled all her ideals. A successful businessman who liked to be put on a pedestal and had dangerous dealings. When she'd heard that, Maddie was embarrassed that she'd never bothered questioning Dalton and his comings and goings any earlier.

One of the servers ran into the kitchen bursting into her reverie which had taken a downward turn. "Maddie, there's something for you out front."

"Why did you not bring it?" Uncle Roberto growled. "And we do not run in the kitchen. Ever!"

"Sorry, Uncle, I was excited." The young man quivered with fear. "I'm afraid it's too heavy to carry by myself."

"Hmmph! Very well, let us see what you have, Maddie."

Checking the ovens first, the uncles waited for Maddie to precede them into the shop. Customers huddled in a group around something on the floor. When they saw her, they parted to reveal the biggest gift basket she had ever seen.

"Are you sure it's for me?"

"It has your name on it," Camille pointed out.

Maddie checked the envelope attached with a ribbon. Madeline Flynn c/o Fournier Bakery. It was for her, all right. But who would send something so lavish?

"Will you open it already?" Camille pleaded.

Excitement poured into her fingers, and Maddie plucked at the strings. The envelope came loose, and carefully she opened it. Inside was a beautiful handwritten card and a signature she knew by heart having seen it in shops and on TV. "I can't believe it!" she gushed and then couldn't say more for the lump in her throat.

Camille grabbed the card. "Wow! It's from Lyra St. Claire. She thanks Maddie for protecting her and saving Dani. She wishes her all the best in her career and offers to help her in any way she can to further it." Camille gasped and handed the card to Uncle Roberto. It passed between the others while Maddie and Camille stared at each other.

"This could be huge." Maddie heard the words as if they'd both said them.

Maddie gulped. It was too much to take in. She'd simply done the right thing, in perhaps a rash way when she thought about it. Certainly, she didn't need a reward for that. But... Lyra St. Claire! It was mind boggling.

"Don't you want to see what she sent?" Camille stared longingly at the delights already visible.

"Yes, of course. Let's do it together."

Camille didn't need even a little begging, and the two of them pulled away the dark cellophane to reveal a treasure trove of baking and chocolates. So much chocolate. There were also several more envelopes. A camera flashed and then several more. Maddie shrunk back from the basket.

"Enough!" boomed Uncle Roberto, making the customers and staff flinch. "Maddie has been through a terrible ordeal. Let her enjoy this moment."

She didn't see how they reacted because Uncle Carlos was already ushering her back to the kitchen and made her sit down. There was some heavy breathing as the other uncles brought the basket and placed it in the corner.

"Take your time to look through it. You do not have to work today," Uncle Roberto insisted as he wiped his sweating brow with a towel.

"I'll have a look later. Right now, I'd rather bake."

He grinned. "Good girl."

Camille hung back. "Are you okay, Maddie? You're so pale."

"I don't know what to make of everything."

Her friend laughed. "Why would you? This has been the weirdest few days, and you've held it together the whole time. You're amazing."

"Anyone would have done the same thing."

"Are you kidding? I'd have been curled into a ball rocking in the corner if this happened to me."

"I doubt that. You let me stay with you and check out that car, which helped the police find Austin."

"Pssh! That was nothing compared to you breaking into the theatre to save Dani. I know you don't like a fuss, but whether you like it or not, you're a hero."

Embarrassed, Maddie laughed. "Don't talk crazy. Now let me get to work, and you can help me open the envelopes later."

Camille punched a fist in the air. "Yes! Although I might have had to hurt you if you didn't include me."

They were still laughing as they pulled on aprons. Normal might not happen right away, but Maddie could see it within reach. There would be no more drama if she could help it.

Something caught her eye out the window. Big Red sat on a large trash can in the alley. He hadn't left her side since she'd got back from the station, and this was as close as he could get while she was at work.

Now there was the real hero.

They stared at each other, and her heart expanded. Contemplating leaving him in Maple Falls where he would be fine living with Gran and have wide-open spaces to explore safely did have merit. She didn't think he'd be happy about it initially, but he'd survive without her. The idea of him not being near made her sad, and the truth was she wouldn't be happy without him near.

Was that selfish or of mutual benefit?

EPILOGUE

In the middle of Camille's apartment, the group was surrounded by gift basket goodies. The uncles had helped her transport it here, and Maddie took the opportunity to thank them for their understanding and kindness during the kidnapping. They brushed off her thanks, looking very pleased all the same.

"I can't believe you left the bakery to come check on me yesterday," she insisted. "As far as I know, it's never happened before."

"You ran out of there like wonder woman, and we saw how scared you were. Even if Camille hadn't explained, we know you well enough that leaving like that meant big trouble." Uncle Roberto cracked his knuckles and glowered. "We've had our share of troubles, and we know how to deal with them. We also agreed that if that poor excuse for a boyfriend was involved in criminal activities, we would make sure he did not hurt you."

She chuckled. "He only hurt my pride at choosing a man who only ever focused on his own interests."

"What exactly was he up to? It had something to do with his job, right?" Camille asked.

Maddie nodded. "He came clean at the station. Not that he had any choice. He was involved in insider trading and honestly thought no one was on to him. Once he realized he was well and truly caught, and Mona was singing like a bird to the world, and trying to blame him for everything, he came clean."

Camille's eyes widened as that sunk in. "And Mona liked the danger of it?"

"Oh, it was more involved than that. Mona has a very dark past and she introduced the parties to each other. If Cleo hadn't got in the way, Dalton was already being targeted by those parties he conned."

"So, it was definitely Mona who killed Cleo?"

Maddie grimaced. "Poor Cleo. She was simply doing her job and Mona dealt with her to get the investigators off their case. She stored the body in a chest and was trying to get it out the door, but wasn't stong enough."

"That must be the scraping you heard."

"Exactly. I guess after thinking on it all night, she decided there was only one option and threw Cleo out the window to cover that she'd been killed earlier, without anticipating that forensics would notice the lack of blood and the burst blood vessels in her eyes which pointed to asphixiation. I suspect the dent at her temple knocked her out so that made the actual killing of Cleo…easy."

A heavy silence settled around the room. Maddie had forgotten that most people were disturbed by such facts. If it weren't for Grandad posing questions she might have felt the same way.

"I think we have all heard enough,"Uncle Joey said loudly. "You are a good person, a great friend to Camille, and very talented, Maddie" he added more gently. "We want you to know you matter to us a great deal and you should come to us at the first sign of any more trouble."

"That's so sweet of you, but I don't think there will be…"

"In fact," Uncle Carlo interrupted. "We were divided about our responsibility, and it took a long time to reach an agreement about telling your grandmother what happened."

She gaped. "You want to phone Gran?"

He shrugged. "Camille told us you couldn't bring yourself to do it."

"I don't want to worry her. Besides, it's all over now," she blustered. "I'll tell her when I go home for Christmas next week."

"There will be a court case for both criminals," Uncle Joey said. "That will be hard and upsetting for you to be reminded of what they did."

"Not to mention seeing a woman killed," Uncle Carlo added.

"She was already dead," Maddie explained. "It wasn't gory at all."

"Gory enough," he insisted. "And you shouldn't have to do it alone."

"I'll be here if she needs me," Camille reminded her father.

"Yes, of course, but all her family should know what is happening."

Maddie's skin prickled just as Big Red ran across the floor, and a knock on the door sounded.

Uncle Joey was closest, so he opened it. "Welcome, dear lady."

Gran strode into the room, looking extremely worried. "Maddie, I believe you have some explaining to do?"

AN HOUR LATER, after unburdening themselves of the whole story, the uncles left laden with some of the goodies, promising Gran they would take care of Maddie.

They'd pulled no punches when they told of the murder and kidnapping from their point of view, and Maddie tried to downplay it, not knowing how successful she was. Eventually the tale was told, and she leaned back against the sofa exhausted.

Sitting next to her, Gran broke the silence. "Camille, you have a lovely father, and your uncles are wonderful too. I'm very grateful that you have taken such good care of my granddaughter."

"Thank you, Mrs. Flynn. We feel very fortunate to have Maddie in our lives." She smiled. "And Big Red."

The cat was draped over Gran's lap—partially. It wasn't a big lap, and he oozed over her slim legs like frosting on a cake.

"Please call me Gran. She is lucky to have you all as well as a job she loves, but I think it's time for her to come home."

Maddie gasped. "I can't leave the bakery, and now that the case is solved I'm safe. Plus, I have the court case to attend."

Gran rarely had a bad word to say about anything. Apparently, this was to be one of those rare times. "But you weren't safe. Plus, you did all those crazy things with little consideration for how it might have gone."

"I did consider it," Maddie argued.

Gran merely raised an eyebrow.

"Okay, I mostly considered my safety and what the repercussions could be. I'm sorry, but it always came back to stopping innocent people getting hurt. If I could prevent that, then I had to try or I couldn't live with myself."

"You're so much like your grandfather," Gran tutted.

Maddie couldn't help smiling. "Thank you."

"It's not always a compliment."

The dryness of the statement wasn't new to Maddie. "I know you think he shouldn't have taught me some things. But if it hadn't been for Grandad, I wouldn't have managed half of what I did yesterday."

Gran sighed. "That may be true, sweetheart, but I still want you to come home. Now that I'm not as young as I used to be, I need more help around the farm."

Maddie took a closer look and her heart sank when she saw the tiredness in Gran's face. "I'm so sorry, I didn't notice you were having difficulties. Are you ill?"

"I'm well enough, so don't give that a second thought. And I don't want you worrying about me." Gran flapped a hand to dismiss the notion.

"So, caring only works one way?" Maddie teased.

"No, but my age gives me seniority on it. Anyway, this is about you and your plans."

Something about Gran's attitude was off. She didn't seem angry or unwell, apart from being tired, but wanted Maddie to come home. Gran always brushed off the topic of ill health, yet she'd intimated that she was getting too frail to manage the small farm. Since she was more like a mother figure, letting her down was the last thing in the world Maddie wanted.

Then it struck her that this was more about keeping her safe. Obviously she'd got a fright when the uncle's called and explained the situation because she came on the very next flight. However, the case was solved, and she had a life here. A life that Gran had encouraged her to pursue. She would need to be firm and see if that made a difference.

"I can't leave right now, even if I wanted to. Maybe we could look at it again in the new year after the trials?"

Gran pursed her lips then shrugged. "I can tell we're not going to resolve this the way I want." Suddenly her eyes twinkled. "Since I didn't know all the details about your shenanigans, I have my friends taking care of the farm for a few days. How about I stay here for Christmas?"

"Really? That would be fantastic. I think we'll be able to get into my apartment tomorrow." She had promised Gran to always come home for Christmas, so this would be her first Christmas spent in New York and she would still be with family. "Do you think you'll be okay to come stay there knowing what happened in the room above?"

"If you're brave enough to go through all of this and still want to live there, then I can certainly manage a few nights." She smiled mischievously. "The Girlz will be shocked by it all and Ethan Tanner might have a thing or two to say about it when you come home."

The 'Girlz' were her close group of friends since childhood and would be on her case to hear all the details the minute they heard. As for her ex-boyfriend…"Maple Falls' sheriff can keep his opinions to himself."

"Just because you two finished, doesn't mean he doesn't still worry about you."

Maddie was well aware of this, because the Girlz had told her. "Well, I don't care to hear if he does."

Gran tutted. "It would be fair to say you've changed a great deal since you became and adult and got a job. The same can be said for Ethan. He's much wiser and has more empathy than he once did."

Was she suggesting that Maddie spend time with the boy who broke her heart? That seemed insensitive and therefore out of character. Maybe she misunderstood, but still felt the need to put her point across. "If that's the case, I'm glad for Maple Falls. However, that changes nothing between him and I."

"That is a shame and I'm sorry to hear it." Gran suddenly smiled serenely. "Now, why don't you show me what's in those envelopes before Camille loses all control?"

Those prickles she got when things weren't quite right ran up her arms and she shook herself like Big Red did when he needed to reset. Whatever Gran was up to, Maddie wasn't going to let worrying about it spoil this night.

Camille reverently handed Maddie the first envelope. Inside was a voucher for a mixer from Cuisine Station, a shop she adored and had yet to purchase anything from. Her hand shook. "This brand is the best in the business and crazy expensive."

"Wow, that's amazing." Camille handed her another envelope. "This one is huge. I have to know what's in it."

Maddie ripped open the flap. "Yay! Two passes to her show, *A Lesson with Lyra!*"

"Please, please say you're taking me!"

"Who else would I take?"

Camille looked pointedly at Gran.

"It's okay, dear." Gran patted her hand. "You deserve lots of treats for taking care of my Maddie so well, and I rarely travel far these days unless I have to." She gave Maddie the side-eye then chuckled. "Come on, I'm dying to know what the rest have in them."

The next hour was fun, despite Gran's insistence about moving home playing on Maddie's mind. It really was impossible to get over the idea that Gran was up to something. Watching closely, she looked to be the epitome of good health, and as soon as Maddie did get home, she would take the time to enlist her friends' help in discovering the truth. Getting to the bottom of a mystery was always interesting, but this one was crucial if she hoped to live in Manhattan without worrying every day about the woman who raised her.

That decided, and with all the treats surrounding them, Maddie finally managed to sit back and take stock of the day.

Camille, Dani, and Lyra were safe. Maddie had helped

solve Cleo Black's death and didn't have to deal with Dalton ever again once the trial finished. She'd won a competition that her idol had judged and on the counter was the trophy to prove it. Camille had gone back to the apartment for Big Red and asked the detective if she could bring the trophy to remind Maddie of something good that happened, despite the murder and Dalton's defection. There was also more chocolate in the room than a person could eat in a year and so many vouchers for appliances she could practically open a small bakery.

And most importantly, her favorite person and Big Red, who was tangled up in ribbons and paper, were right here celebrating with her.

It was going to be a great Christmas and she'd try not to worry about going home for good until after that.

Thanks so much for reading Sugar and Sliced the prequel to the Maple Lane Mysteries series. I hope you enjoyed it!

If you did…
1 Help other people find this book by leaving a review.

2 Sign up for my new release e-mail https://dl.bookfunnel. com/s7ae15d3fx so you can find out about the next book as soon as it's available.

3 Come like my Facebook page.

4 Visit my website for the very best deals.

5 Keep reading for an excerpt from Book 1 in the series, Apple Pie and Arsenic.

APPLE PIE AND ARSENIC

When Maddie sighed, Bernie Davis shot her a sympathetic grin. "Nearly home, love. It's a shame you couldn't come back more often. With not being so well over the winter, Gran's sorely missed you. "

Was there a touch of censure in his statement? She wouldn't be at all surprised. They'd chatted about all sorts of things that weren't too personal, apart from the initial "'Hi, how are you?'" Clearly, the time had come for him to ask what the rest of the town would want to know. As the only taxi driver in town and the odd-job man for most of the population, it was expected that he would have the latest gossip on anyone entering or leaving Maple Falls. Especially if the passenger was one of their own.

Maddie sighed again. It was probably best to get a plausible response out there and avoid the question being asked 10,914 times, even if it annoyed her to have everyone know her business. Like it or not, Maple Falls was probably never going to change regarding that.

"It *has* been too long. I've been working hard and saving for my own bakery. A vacation hasn't been possible."

Bernie grinned. "Well, you're here now. Gran's been telling us how well you're doing, even after changing jobs. A bakery of your own in New York? You'll be more famous around here than you already are when that gets out."

Maddie brushed that aside, still feeling awkward at receiving praise from an entire town; especially when they'd expected more from the business degree scholarship she'd been awarded.

When she'd left college, she believed aiming for success in that arena was what she should be doing. After all, her marks in business studies had been what got her the scholarship. But as soon as the degree cooled in her hand and she was working her very first job, Maddie knew it was a mistake—a big one. Madeline Flynn was not made for sitting behind a desk. No, she was a working-with-her-hands type of girl.

She should have known, and maybe deep down she had but hadn't wanted to admit it. At the time, accepting that scholarship meant she felt obligated to make it work and desperately made herself fit into that world. Every day was torture. Even the wonderful outcomes when she helped people achieve their dreams didn't make her feel the way she did when she was baking. But baking was a hobby, not something she could make a career of. Or so she'd thought.

Going from a well-paid job to starting at the ground level in a bakery would be a terrible waste. For two years she told herself that. Finally, when she was completely miserable with her life, and despite a steady boyfriend who thought she was insane to consider throwing away her career, she knew the time had come to stop working at something she felt no passion for and she had called Gran.

Naturally, her grandmother hadn't said a word about the waste of a degree, wasn't at all surprised by Maddie's change of heart, and certainly didn't care what people thought.

When the opportunity to change careers arose, it was through a chance meeting with a woman who came to Maddie seeking help with marketing for a future venture. A venture that Maddie was naturally interested in since it revolved around owning a bakery. This shared dream ensured they became good friends and when Camille told her bosses at the bakery where she worked, all about Maddie, they'd called her in for an interview.

The sights and smells of the famous French bakery were heavenly, and Maddie's heart beat with the passion she'd been keeping under wraps. This was the life she wanted. Whether it was due to Camille's good word or her own over-the-top delight, the owners offered her a job starting at the bottom. It was a huge leap of faith for a family business that didn't generally hire outsiders, and Maddie liked to believe she was deserving of that faith.

Her heart knew it was the right choice, and with Gran's blessing, she'd jumped at the chance and never regretted her decision. However, a residual embarrassment lingered at being seen as a failure around Maple Falls.

"What's been happening here, Bernie?" She changed the subject.

"The usual. People stepping on toes and then having a drink over their apologies."

"Nothing new, then?"

They laughed together at the notion that Maple Falls might change in any way. Situated twenty miles south of the bigger town of Destiny, Maple Falls was a lot older, had charm in bucket-loads and almost everything a person needed.

Bernie suddenly frowned. "There is one bit of unsavory news. The mayor has been under fire from an anonymous source. I know Denise is a friend of yours, so I thought you might like to know she's struggling a bit."

Maddie had been happy to let Bernie talk while she enjoyed the scenery, but now he had her full attention. Denise was a lovely, big-hearted person, so to hear she was being harassed was upsetting. "How do you mean?"

"It's stuff in the paper and flyers appearing all over town about how she isn't living up to election promises of bringing in more tourists or boosting the economy in other ways."

"Surely Maple Falls is doing great for a small town?"

His brow creased at her tone. "Hey, don't shoot the messenger. I'm doing fine and so are most people, but gossip can spread and we do have a few members of our community that don't exactly share the same spirit as the rest."

Bernie was being tactful, but they both knew whom he was referring to. Maddie would be keeping an eye out for them and as much as she might hate confrontation she wouldn't stand by and let Denise be hurt. She sighed. Not even home yet and she was already enmeshed in a Maple Falls drama.

"Sorry. I'm just surprised, because Denise has already done so much good."

He nodded as they crested the last hill, and there, stretching out before them, was the town itself. Once more, a peaceful feeling settled over her.

To the left were the vineyards. Row upon neat row stretched out to the mountains, with the small lake sparkling at their base. To the right was farmland. Rich and fertile, the land around Maple Falls was a beautiful myriad of colors that never dimmed even in winter.

At the bottom of the hill and on the outskirts of Maple Falls, Bernie slowed considerably. It was something people did automatically, even before the 30-mph sign was in view, because the old town was spectacularly beautiful and worth an unhurried look.

Especially now, in her best season, anyone who had a heart was bewitched by Maple Falls. Spring was when the old girl shrugged off the darker shades of winter and burst out into the colors of the rainbow, when every garden in every street blossomed as if in competition.

Maddie almost laughed again. There was no denying that the residents could be very competitive, from gardens to the annual spring fair, where they could showcase everything from flowers to baking, crafts to furniture making. Summer heralded the music festivals and farmers' markets, while fall was full of family fun, harvest festivals, and corn mazes to delight the young and old. Finally, there was the winter carnival and the time when Christmas decorating took center stage. There was always a season and an unwritten opportunity to go one better. Of course, it was all done good-naturedly.

A canopy of big-leafed maple trees shaded the main street and many of the ones intersecting it. They were enormous specimens of the Oregon native, some even reaching close to their top height of sixty feet.

The founding fathers' properties still stood interspersed along the main street with the businesses, the sheriff's department, and the fire station. Out of the three brothers who had founded Maple Falls in 1880, one descendant,

Mickey Findlay, occupied one, while the others had long ago been sold to the town. Of those, one was now the doctor's office and a small pharmacy; the other was home to the Mayor's office and the community center.

They were impressive buildings which had been studiously maintained through the years. The community center was a hive of activity, serving as a meeting place for the older generation, who Gran presided over like a queen bee.

Maddie hadn't lived here for several years, although she had come home for most of the holidays until she changed jobs. That was when the questions about her use of the scholarship veiled thinly with disapproval began. Although a few things had changed, trees had grown, families had come and gone, businesses opened or closed, Gran and her best friend Angel were what always drew her back.

When they reached the center of town, a wave of nostalgia hit her. Here was a place, despite being the town's hub, which had the quiet grace only a small town could convey. The well-worn sidewalks and roads were spotlessly clean, as were the front yards of the locals who were rightly proud to live here.

It wasn't quiet because there were people around, but after living and working in the hustle and bustle of New York for a few years, for Maddie this was a direct contrast. People acknowledged each other. They stopped to chat and really listened to what a person had to say.

It was a relief to know the place where she'd grown up was still the same, and that the woman who'd raised her would be waiting to welcome her with open arms. Gran was more like a mother than a grandmother. She had taken Maddie in without hesitation when Maddie's mother had left town for a faster-paced life. With no father on the scene, maybe her grandparents had felt they had little choice, but they'd never made Maddie feel anything but loved.

Coming home meant so many things, but at the heart of her emotions was what the two of them shared. Because they were so alike in their love of baking and friends, it had been a wrench for Maddie to leave. And even at twenty-eight, it still was.

Maple Falls was where her heart lay when it came to a place to live, but she had been on the cusp of something really great in New York. Having looked into buying a bakery with a friend, she was so close to having her dream come true, she could taste it. Pun intended. Then Gran's SOS had come, and there was no other choice for Maddie but to come home to Maple Falls, because her feelings about letting people down were no match for how much she would do for Gran.

As they drove down Maple Lane, the main street, people waved as they went about their business. Isaac Carter ran the local diner, and he was writing the day's specials on the board outside. Maude Oliver, president of the Maple Falls Country Club and secretary of the town board, stopped poking the vegetables on display at Janet Mitchell's grocery story, and Jed Clayton, a sweet old man, was walking through the park, whistling for his dog. The grapevine would already be well into overdrive to say she was back, but there was nothing to be done about that.

Then they were turning into Plum Place. Now, this really was home. Maddie had walked all over town more times than she could remember, but this was her street, and she knew every inch of it.

Everything looked the same except for one of the shops. From the front, it appeared neglected compared to the others. From this side, it was almost derelict, which would not go down well with the town board.

Then they were past it and pulling into her grandmother's driveway. Wisteria graced the porch, the purple flowers hanging like succulent bunches of grapes. The rocker—exactly how old it was made an often-repeated conversation piece, since it had been there for three generations at least—was moving gently in the breeze.

Gran appeared in the doorway as if she'd been watching for Maddie. Knowing Gran, she probably had been. A marvel at nearly seventy, she'd recently admitted she was getting too old to maintain the family home she'd inherited from her parents. After a major bout of bronchitis last winter, she'd decided to sell. That had been a shock, but as much as it tugged her heartstrings, Maddie was here to help her find a new home. It was the least she could do.

The wonderful family bakery where Maddie currently worked with Camille, was in the heart of Manhattan and did a flourishing trade. In fact, they were one of the busiest in the city, and they needed every pair of hands right now. They'd granted her a week for this unplanned break, and if that wasn't enough time to get the ball rolling, Maddie wasn't sure what would happen. The one thing she did know was Gran wouldn't choose the first place she saw. She was a thinker, and that generally took time.

It was difficult to think of Gran as old. Her ramrod-straight back and salt and pepper hair tucked neatly into a bun looked the same as they had for years, as did her smile and floral apron. Both were her trademarks, and one rarely appeared without the other.

"Hello, darling," she called out as Maddie got out of the taxi. "Good timing. I've just pulled an apple pie from the oven."

CHAPTER Two

Maddie could smell the pie from where she was standing, and Bernie had a hopeful glint in his eyes. Once you'd tried Gran's baking, nothing ever tasted as good.

People came from miles away, paying her to make birthday cakes and delicious baked treats, and had done so for years. More often than not, she took less money than she should, and it was agreed by all her customers that whatever treat she made and whatever she charged was certainly worth it.

Bernie opened the back of his van and carefully pulled out a large cage and set it on the grass beside the driveway. Once he'd taken her bag to the porch, Maddie gave him his fare and added a hefty tip for his trouble. Not everyone wanted a cat like hers in their vehicle, but Bernie never raised an eyebrow, and he always did the lifting, which was a marked difference from New York City cabbies.

"Just you wait a minute," Gran said to Bernie.

He grinned in anticipation. No-one went away from here without something to eat.

Then she gave Maddie a hug. They hugged hard, the way Maddie had been taught. The Flynn mantra was "hug someone like you mean it, or don't bother."

She savored the smell of apples and cinnamon, which was Gran's brand of perfume. One that couldn't be bought. One that meant love and home.

Gran smiled, a little misty-eyed, when they let go and went inside to fix a plate for Bernie.

Big Red yawned as Maddie opened his cage, then jumped out onto the grass as gracefully as he was able. "I'll be inside," she told him, giving his arched back the expected scratch.

The big Maine Coon gave her a disgruntled look, stretched, and with a flick of his tail sashayed over to the shade of the maple tree that dominated the front yard.

Poor boy. She could appreciate that his trip had been a

C. A. PHIPPS

great deal less comfortable than hers. Even with the air conditioning on, the taxi had been hot, and what the plane had been like for him, she hated to think. He wasn't a cage kind of animal, and he would only get into it with great reluctance and many treats.

For such a short visit, she would ordinarily leave Big Red in the kennels, but they'd let her know last time that Big Red wasn't welcome back—something to do with asserting his authority overzealously with his peers.

Despite Gran's ill health, a couple of incidents involving her ex-boyfriend who was involved in dodgy dealings made getting away from Manhattan more enticing. However, Maddie refused to give that any head space at all. It was wonderful to be home.

Gran came out with the covered plate and handed it to Bernie who looked as excited as a child at Christmas. "I'll expect that plate back next time you're passing," she said.

"Much appreciated and I will." He touched his cap and carried it carefully back to his car as if he held precious gems.

"Welcome home," Gran called out to Big Red. She gave a wry smile as Maddie joined her on the porch. "He looks cross. I guess he'll come in when he's ready."

"You know him so well." Maddie grinned. "Now, tell me how you really are. I've been so worried since your call. I'm sorry it's taken a couple of weeks to get here."

Gran waved her apron at the fuss. "I'm doing great, and I'd have been pleased to see you any time you could make it. I certainly didn't expect you to be on the next plane."

Maddie had thought Gran might resist her help when she'd called to say she was on her way home. When no resistance was forthcoming, she'd assumed the worst. "I'm so glad you're doing a lot better than I was anticipating."

"Goodness, did I give the impression I was on death's

144

door?" Gran chuckled. "The bronchitis was bad, but the cough's nearly gone. Although, I do admit that the packing seems to have made me a little maudlin."

Maddie put an arm around her as they walked through to the kitchen, leaving her bag for later. "It's only natural. This is your home, and you've lived here all your life."

Gran squeezed her waist. "Like you."

They were the same height of 5'7" and had similar builds. When Maddie looked at pictures of her childhood and compared them to Gran's, they looked so alike that they could have been sisters. For a child without parents, that was a big deal.

"Yes, that's true, but I've also lived other places now. Not that I won't shed a tear or two when you sell, but I'm sure it won't be as painful for me as it will be for you."

"That you understand means a great deal to me, sweetheart. I sure hope you don't mind using your vacation time to help me out. I hate to be a bother."

"Psssh! You could never be a bother, so don't give it a thought. Where else would I take a vacation? Plus, I wouldn't have let you do this by yourself. Real estate agents can be hard to deal with, and you'll want to get a good price."

"I know you don't take nearly enough vacation time, but I'm grateful you're here now. The thought of tackling this on my own was pretty terrifying," Gran sniffed, pinching the bridge of her nose. "Your granddad took care of the big things. Tea?"

They might occasionally talk about being upset, but being staunch was also a major factor in their DNA. They were tough, and they liked it that way.

Gran's daughter, aka Maddie's mom, had been a handful, according to Gran. Ava Flynn broke both their hearts when she left, even though they'd tried every way they could think of to show her they loved her. It had gnawed at the young

145

Maddie, and she knew it had affected Gran because she would sometimes catch her staring at a photo of Granddad and Mom.

Fifteen years later, Maddie's mother was still missed, but they had moved on from being sad, and tea was still the magic potion for everything. Being an Anglophile, anything English was close to Gran's heart, but tea was her main legacy from her parents. Born and raised in Liverpool, they had emigrated to America when Gran was a teenager, but she'd never forgotten her roots.

Her kitchen had shelves filled with an assortment of bric-a-brac that all in some way represented England. Single sets of matching cups and saucers with side plates, tea canisters with pictures of the royal family adorning them, and many teapots in a similar vein were lovingly dusted on a regular basis.

"I'd love a cup," Maddie said. "In fact, I need one. The traffic was horrible until we got past Portland. I hope one day they build an airport in Oregon closer to Maple Falls that's big enough to handle passenger planes." The one in Destiny was for light planes and helicopters, all privately owned.

Gran carefully took two cups and saucers from the shelf, along with side plates, while Maddie filled the kettle. It was an old relic passed down by Gran's mother, who had died long before Maddie was born and had instilled in her daughter the art of tea-making. Each set of cups and saucers was different and often had not been purchased together.

Over time, Gran had accumulated more than a dozen sets. If a person came for tea more than a couple of times, a particular set became theirs. Maddie always used the one with a pink rose, while Gran's favorite had lilacs.

"I haven't been to Portland since you were last home. Actually, it doesn't interest me to go far these days."

Maddie was plugging in the electric kettle that was as important as the best brand of tea that Gran insisted on using. She turned quickly. "You'd tell me if you were still unwell, wouldn't you?"

"Of course I would. Why do you ask?"

"You've always loved your weekly jaunts to anywhere the buses or trains would take you, and you've said more than once that you'd have to be taken out of this house in a coffin to get you to leave."

Gran laughed. "I did say that didn't I? But things change, and I have to be realistic. I'm no longer a spring chicken. I'm also thinking about handing over the leadership of the community group to some younger blood."

"What? No way. Those ladies depend on you to liven things up around here." The club had been founded by Gran and a couple of her best friends, and they were forever searching for places to go and speakers who loved interesting things.

"That's the thing," Gran said. "They need to change it up. This is the twenty-first century, for goodness' sake. There must be other things to do that I've never heard of."

Maddie snorted at the idea of that group of women "changing things up". They were the happiest bunch of older men and women, doing what they loved, but perhaps not all as open to change as Gran.

Still, the club had played a big part in Gran's life, especially after Maddie left. Since Gran had never learned to drive, a bus or taxi was the only way for her to get around unless someone offered her a ride to Destiny. Every month, she organized the community group jaunt to somewhere as a day trip, as well as their speakers. It was a shock for Maddie to hear her giving up on it. Who would take that task on now?

Gran liked to be busy, and she also walked for miles. At

least, she always had. She looked so healthy and fit, Maddie had a hard time thinking of her as either old or sickly.

"It's been good for me to be the president for so long, and it was something to keep me busy while you were away, but I'm over it," Gran continued. "I've been everywhere several dozen times, and now I can honestly say that staying around home is far more appealing."

"Except you're moving."

"That's true, but a home is whom you fill it with, not wood and nails."

Maddie's eyes prickled with tears, and she felt a distinct twinge of regret at the idea of someone else living here. Still, this was Gran's decision, not hers. She sucked up her sadness and smiled as she warmed the teapot and added English Breakfast tea leaves, their favorite, then filled it with boiling water.

"It's so nice to be back in Maple Falls and out of the rat race, but I only have a week, which means we need to get on to finding you a new place, pronto."

They sat at the old oak table, which had been scrubbed so often that it was now much paler than it had started out. Gran pushed a pile of brochures and papers at Maddie, as well as a large slice of pie. It was still warm, and Maddie took a forkful, then closed her eyes.

"Mmmm. I've missed your baking."

"I'm sure that after all that training in a French patisserie, yours is just as good, if not better."

Maddie tilted her head, savoring the pie. "Not quite. But it's getting close."

Honesty had been a strong part of growing up with Gran, who couldn't abide lies, so there was no point in false modesty. But how could you compare your own food with that of the woman whose recipes were loved by so many, and from whom you had begun to learn your craft? Gran had founded and fueled Maddie's passion for baking, a passion that had never waned.

She took another bite of pie. Yep, this was heaven on a plate. Gran was sitting across from her, patiently waiting for a decent pause, or for her to finish, whichever came first. Reluctantly, she put down her fork and spread out the brochures. Selling the family home was the right thing to do, but that didn't make it easier. These walls held so many memories—most of them happy.

Her heart sank at the sight of so many places to view. "Do you want to see all of these?"

"I've circled a few that may be of interest, but I wanted to discuss another option."

Maddie knew that tone. Gran could be very persuasive in general, but when she adopted that tone, you could bet something you weren't ready for was about to hit you squarely in the face and would probably stick like strawberry jam.

She took a few sips of the strong brew then a deep breath. "Okay. I'm ready. Tell me what you're up to."

Gran grimaced. "You're being a little dramatic, and it's not like I'd force anything on you."

She completely ignored Maddie's open mouth at the unfamiliar censure and tapped the top brochure.

"Here's the retirement community Angel took me to visit. It's quite nice, but they have a 'no overnight guests' policy, meaning you couldn't stay with me. I don't like that idea one bit." She turned it over and replaced it with several more. "There are these."

She flicked each one by Maddie's nose. Very fast. Maddie waited for the bomb to drop, and fortunately she only had to suffer the blur of papers for another few seconds.

"Then there's this. Now, I know you have your own plans,

but please don't say no right away. Read it, go see it, then decide. Okay?"

Gran had begun to look jittery as she waved the paper in front of Maddie.

"Good gravy. How bad can this be? My nerves are turning to custard."

The slightly wrinkled chin lifted defiantly. "It's not bad at all. In fact, it's a wonderful opportunity if you can see the potential like I do."

Maddie pulled the paper from her hand so quickly that a small corner of it remained in Gran's fingertips. The front of the brochure was graced with a picture of a familiar block of four stores. A red rectangle was around one of them—the one Maddie noticed looked unkempt. At the end of the block, it not only sat on the main street of Maple Lane but backed onto Plum Place. Just up the road.

"I don't understand. You've decided to sell the house because it's too much. Why would you want a shop?"

Gran's eyebrows shot up. "For a bakery, of course. If I buy the shop, that one there"—she pointed at the red one— "it comes with a two-bedroom apartment upstairs, and since they all back onto our road, they have small yards of their own. It's a bit tired, but we've redecorated this house, so I know we can do the same to the shop and the apartment to make it just as lovely."

Maddie shut her gaping mouth with a snap. "You're not making sense. You can't manage a shop!"

Gran looked astounded, as if Maddie had stupidly missed the point. But what, exactly, *was* the point?

"No, I couldn't, but you could."

"Me?" Maddie was as confused as confectioners' sugar pretending to be frosting.

"For goodness' sake. I'm not speaking a foreign language. Isn't that your dream? To open your own bakery?"

Still feeling as if she were in an alternate universe, Maddie nodded. "Sure, but not here."

Gran sniffed. "Why not? I'd have thought Maple Lane was a perfect location."

Maddie had no idea what had brought on this weird conversation, but she wasn't liking where it was going. "It would be if I didn't plan on opening a bakery in New York City someday soon."

"It would be much cheaper to open one here."

Maddie tried to keep the frustration out of her voice. "That's true, but I don't have the money yet to buy a shop outright."

"Don't get prickly. I appreciate all of that. First, the owner is desperate to sell, so it's going for a song. Second, what if I put money in? I have savings. Or I could buy the whole thing outright with the sale from this place, and you could pay me back when you can."

Maddie was stunned for a moment. "No, Gran, I'm not taking your money. You've done so much for me already."

"I've done what family does when they love each other, nothing more. Anyway, you know everything I have will come to you when I'm pushing up daisies."

Maddie knew Gran wanted her back home, but this talk of not being around was scary, and it made her think once more that Gran might be sick and not telling her.

"You're not putting all your money into something that has no guarantee of success. I'll come home if you need me, but I'm not buying a shop in Maple Falls."

Gran looked down for a moment. When she raised her head, she tried to smile but failed miserably. "I totally understand. You should follow your heart and do what's right for you. Let's not talk about it anymore today. We can discuss more options tomorrow. Maybe I should rethink the retirement community."

Minutes ago, Gran had been excited about the prospect of going into business together, and now she looked utterly despondent. Was Maddie the worst granddaughter ever? She sure felt like it. Each bite turned to sawdust in her mouth.

This wasn't a good start. If Gran had her heart set on the business and the apartment, then one week would never be enough to talk her into something else. Clearly it couldn't be the retirement community if even the thought of it made her miserable.

A germ of an idea took hold, and Maddie grasped it with both hands. The shops had been there for decades, and the one Gran was talking about looked truly awful from the outside. The inside had to be as bad. Probably worse. Maybe if they took a look at it and Gran saw how much they'd have to do to get it up and running, she would change her mind.

Pleased with that idea and hopeful that they could find a nice place for Gran afterwards, she smiled. "On second thought, if you think it's worth our time, let's go see this place. After all, a look can't hurt, can it?"

Gran's face lit up once more. "Really? Now?"

Maddie raised an eyebrow. "Maybe I could finish my tea and pie?"

Gran leaned back with an air of satisfaction. "Take as long as you like. I'll give the agent a call in a minute. Should I say to meet her there in half an hour?"

Maddie spluttered her mouthful of tea over the pristine white tablecloth. She had the feeling that she'd just been played, but she couldn't think of anything to say in the face of such eagerness. She dabbed at the mess with a napkin while Gran brought the phone to the table.

She'd never made Maddie feel anything but wanted and loved, and doing anything to make Gran happy had never been an issue. Unfortunately, this felt like a step too far.

As soon as her plate was empty, Gran dialed the number

and it was then that Maddie realized whom she was calling. They both knew the owner of the local real estate business, and the thought of seeing Virginia Bolton, let alone discussing business with her, was enough to make Maddie's insides turn to jelly.

What a morning, and it wasn't done yet.

Need to read more?
Get your copy of Apple Pie and Arsenic today!

RECIPES

These recipes are ones I use all the time and have come down the generations from my mum, grandmother, and some I have adapted from other recipes. Also, I now have my husband's grandmother's recipe book. Exciting! I'll be bringing some of them to life very soon.

Just a wee reminder, that I am a New Zealander. Occasionally I may have missed converting into ounces and pounds for my American readers.

My apologies for that, and please let me know—if you do try them—how they turn out.

Cheryl x

RASPBERRY MUFFINS

Ingredients

2 cups self-raising flour
½ cup castor sugar
1 egg
¾ cup milk
1 tsp vanilla essence
100 g / 7 tbsp butter
1 tbsp golden syrup
12 tsp raspberry jam
12 tsp cream cheese
Confectioners' sugar for dusting

Instructions

1 Heat oven to 220C / 428F and grease 12 medium muffin tins.

2 Into a bowl, sift flour into a bowl and add sugar. Stir.

3 Beat egg and add milk, vanilla essence and melted butter. Stir.

4 Pour wet mixture into dry mixture and stir until smooth.

5 Spoon into pans to halfway. In the center add a tsp of jam and a tsp of cream cheese. Cover evenly with remaining mixture.

6 Bake for 12 minutes and cool for 5 minutes.

7 Dust with confectioners' sugar.

RASPBERRY MERINGUE SLICE

Ingredients
4½ ozs / 125g Butter
3/4 cup Caster Sugar
2 egg separated
1¾ cup Plain Flour
1½ tsp Baking Powder
¼ cup extra Caster Sugar
1 cup coconut
1 tsp vanilla essence
½ cup raspberry jam

Instructions
1 Preheat oven to 180°C.
2 Grease a 20cm x 30cm tin and line with baking paper.
3 Cream softened butter and Sugar until light and fluffy.
4 Beat in egg yolks one at a time.
5 Add sifted flour and Baking Powder. Mix well until it binds loosely and press evenly into tin.
6 Spread the raspberry jam evenly over the mixture.
7 In a clean bowl beat the egg whites and sugar until stiff.

8 Gently fold in the coconut and vanilla and spread over the jam.

9 Bake for 30 minutes or until lightly brown.

10 Cool slightly before cutting into squares. Remove from tin when cold.

ALSO BY C. A. PHIPPS

The Maple Lane Cozy Mysteries

Sugar and Sliced - Maple Lane Prequel

Apple Pie and Arsenic

Bagels and Blackmail

Cookies and Chaos

Doughnuts and Disaster

Eclairs and Extortion

Fudge and Frenemies

Gingerbread and Gunshots

Honey Cake and Homicide - preorder now!

Midlife Potions - Paranormal Cozy Mysteries

Witchy Awakening

Witchy Hot Spells

Witchy Flash Back

Witchy Bad Blood - preorder now!

Beagle Diner Cozy Mysteries

Beagles Love Cupcake Crimes

Beagles Love Steak Secrets

Beagles Love Muffin But Murder

Beagles Love Layer Cake Lies

The Cozy Café Mysteries

Sweet Saboteur

Candy Corruption

Mocha Mayhem

Berry Betrayal

Deadly Desserts

Please note: Most are also available in paperback and some in audio.

Remember to join Cheryl's Cozy Mystery newsletter.
There's a free recipe book waiting for you. ;-)
Cheryl also writes romance as Cheryl Phipps.

ACKNOWLEDGMENTS

Thanks in bucket loads to my amazing Beta readers, Bernadette Cinkoske, Linda Brown, Suzanne Nelson, and Barbara Wellnitz, whose support means so much to me. Editors rarely get everything perfect, so it is these wonderful women whose collective pointers, fact and grammar checks, help to make each book better.

ABOUT THE AUTHOR

'Life is a mystery. Let's follow the clues together.'

C. A. Phipps is a USA Today best-selling author from beautiful New Zealand. Cheryl is an empty-nester living in a quiet suburb with her wonderful husband, 'himself'. With an extended family to keep her busy when she's not writing, there is just enough space for a crazy mixed breed dog who stole her heart! She enjoys family times, baking, and her quest for the perfect latte.

Check out her website http://caphipps.com

facebook.com/authorcaphipps
x.com/CherylAPhipps
instagram.com/caphippsauthor

Made in the USA
Middletown, DE
18 August 2024

59390257R00102